## THE PELICAN SHAKESPEARE

### GENERAL EDITOR ALFRED HARBAGE

### THE WINTER'S TALE

# WILLIAM SHAKESPEARE

# THE WINTER'S TALE

EDITED BY BALDWIN MAXWELL

PENGUIN BOOKS

PENGUIN BOOKS
Published by the Penguin Group
Viking Penguin, a division of Penguin Books USA Inc.,
375 Hudson Street, New York, New York 10014, U.S.A.
Penguin Books Ltd, 27 Wrights Lane,
London W8 5TZ, England
Penguin Books Australia Ltd, Ringwood,
Victoria, Australia
Penguin Books Canada Ltd, 10 Alcorn Avenue, Suite 300,
Toronto, Ontario, Canada M4V 3B2
Penguin Books (N.Z.) Ltd, 182–190 Wairau Road,
Auckland 10, New Zealand

Penguin Books Ltd, Registered Offices:
Harmondsworth, Middlesex, England

First published in *The Pelican Shakespeare* 1956
This revised edition first published 1971

15   17   19   20   18   16   14

Copyright © Penguin Books, Inc., 1956, 1971
All rights reserved

Library of Congress catalog card number: 70-98379
ISBN 0 14 071404 9

Printed in the United States of America
Set in Monotype Ehrhardt

# CONTENTS

# PUBLISHER'S NOTE

Soon after the thirty-eight volumes forming *The Pelican Shakespeare* had been published, they were brought together in *The Complete Pelican Shakespeare*. The editorial revisions and new textual features are explained in detail in the General Editor's Preface to the one-volume edition. They have all been incorporated in the present volume. The following should be mentioned in particular:

The lines are not numbered in arbitrary units. Instead all lines are numbered which contain a word, phrase, or allusion explained in the glossarial notes. In the occasional instances where there is a long stretch of unannotated text, certain lines are numbered in italics to serve the conventional reference purpose.

The intrusive and often inaccurate place-headings inserted by early editors are omitted (as is becoming standard practise), but for the convenience of those who miss them, an indication of locale now appears as first item in the annotation of each scene.

In the interest of both elegance and utility, each speech-prefix is set in a separate line when the speaker's lines are in verse, except when these words form the second half of a pentameter line. Thus the verse form of the speech is kept visually intact, and turned-over lines are avoided. What is printed as verse and what is printed as prose has, in general, the authority of the original texts. Departures from the original texts in this regard have only the authority of editorial tradition and the judgment of the Pelican editors; and, in a few instances, are admittedly arbitrary.

# SHAKESPEARE AND
# HIS STAGE

William Shakespeare was christened in Holy Trinity
Church, Stratford-upon-Avon, April 26, 1564. His birth
is traditionally assigned to April 23. He was the eldest of
four boys and two girls who survived infancy in the family
of John Shakespeare, glover and trader of Henley Street,
and his wife Mary Arden, daughter of a small landowner
of Wilmcote. In 1568 John was elected Bailiff (equivalent
to Mayor) of Stratford, having already filled the minor
municipal offices. The town maintained for the sons of the
burgesses a free school, taught by a university graduate
and offering preparation in Latin sufficient for university
entrance; its early registers are lost, but there can be little
doubt that Shakespeare received the formal part of his
education in this school.

On November 27, 1582, a license was issued for the
marriage of William Shakespeare (aged eighteen) and Ann
Hathaway (aged twenty-six), and on May 26, 1583, their
child Susanna was christened in Holy Trinity Church.
The inference that the marriage was forced upon the youth
is natural but not inevitable; betrothal was legally binding
at the time, and was sometimes regarded as conferring
conjugal rights. Two additional children of the marriage,
the twins Hamnet and Judith, were christened on Feb-
ruary 2, 1585. Meanwhile the prosperity of the elder
Shakespeares had declined, and William was impelled to
seek a career outside Stratford.

The tradition that he spent some time as a country

teacher is old but unverifiable. Because of the absence of records his early twenties are called the "lost years," and only one thing about them is certain – that at least some of these years were spent in winning a place in the acting profession. He may have begun as a provincial trouper, but by 1592 he was established in London and prominent enough to be attacked. In a pamphlet of that year, *Groats-worth of Wit*, the ailing Robert Greene complained of the neglect which university writers like himself had suffered from actors, one of whom was daring to set up as a playwright:

> ... an vpstart Crow, beautified with our feathers, that with his *Tygers hart wrapt in a Players hyde*, supposes he is as well able to bombast out a blanke verse as the best of you: and beeing an absolute *Iohannes fac totum*, is in his owne conceit the onely Shake-scene in a countrey.

The pun on his name, and the parody of his line "O tiger's heart wrapped in a woman's hide" (*3 Henry VI*), pointed clearly to Shakespeare. Some of his admirers protested, and Henry Chettle, the editor of Greene's pamphlet, saw fit to apologize:

> ... I am as sory as if the originall fault had beene my fault, because my selfe haue seene his demeanor no lesse ciuill than he excelent in the qualitie he professes: Besides, diuers of worship haue reported his vprightnes of dealing, which argues his honesty, and his facetious grace in writting, that approoues his Art. (Prefatory epistle, *Kind-Harts Dreame*)

The plague closed the London theatres for many months in 1592–94, denying the actors their livelihood. To this period belong Shakespeare's two narrative poems, *Venus and Adonis* and *The Rape of Lucrece*, both dedicated to the Earl of Southampton. No doubt the poet was rewarded with a gift of money as usual in such cases, but he did no further dedicating and we have no reliable information on whether Southampton, or anyone else, became his regular patron. His sonnets, first mentioned in 1598 and published without his consent in 1609, are intimate without being explicitly autobiographical. They seem to commemorate the poet's friendship with an idealized youth, rivalry with a more favored poet, and love affair with a dark mistress; and his bitterness when the mistress betrays him in conjunction with the friend; but it is difficult to decide precisely what the "story" is, impossible to decide whether it is fictional or true. The true distinction of the sonnets, at least of those not purely conventional, rests in the universality of the thoughts and moods they express, and in their poignancy and beauty.

In 1594 was formed the theatrical company known until 1603 as the Lord Chamberlain's men, thereafter as the King's men. Its original membership included, besides Shakespeare, the beloved clown Will Kempe and the famous actor Richard Burbage. The company acted in various London theatres and even toured the provinces, but it is chiefly associated in our minds with the Globe Theatre built on the south bank of the Thames in 1599. Shakespeare was an actor and joint owner of this company (and its Globe) through the remainder of his creative years. His plays, written at the average rate of two a year, together with Burbage's acting won it its place of leadership among the London companies.

Individual plays began to appear in print, in editions both honest and piratical, and the publishers became increasingly aware of the value of Shakespeare's name on the title pages. As early as 1598 he was hailed as the leading English dramatist in the *Palladis Tamia* of Francis Meres:

As *Plautus* and *Seneca* are accounted the best for Comedy and Tragedy among the Latines, so *Shakespeare* among the English is the most excellent in both kinds for the stage: for Comedy, witnes his *Gentlemen of Verona*, his *Errors*, his *Loue labors lost*, his *Loue labours wonne* [at one time in print but no longer extant, at least under this title], his *Midsummers night dream*, & his *Merchant of Venice*; for Tragedy, his *Richard the 2*, *Richard the 3*, *Henry the 4*, *King Iohn*, *Titus Andronicus*, and his *Romeo and Iuliet*.

9

The note is valuable both in indicating Shakespeare's prestige and in helping us to establish a chronology. In the second half of his writing career, history plays gave place to the great tragedies; and farces and light comedies gave place to the problem plays and symbolic romances. In 1623, seven years after his death, his former fellow-actors, John Heminge and Henry Condell, cooperated with a group of London printers in bringing out his plays in collected form. The volume is generally known as the First Folio.

Shakespeare had never severed his relations with Stratford. His wife and children may sometimes have shared his London lodgings, but their home was Stratford. His son Hamnet was buried there in 1596, and his daughters Susanna and Judith were married there in 1607 and 1616 respectively. (His father, for whom he had secured a coat of arms and thus the privilege of writing himself gentleman, died in 1601, his mother in 1608.) His considerable earnings in London, as actor-sharer, part owner of the Globe, and playwright, were invested chiefly in Stratford property. In 1597 he purchased for £60 New Place, one of the two most imposing residences in the town. A number of other business transactions, as well as minor episodes in his career, have left documentary records. By 1611 he was in a position to retire, and he seems gradually to have withdrawn from theatrical activity in order to live in Stratford. In March, 1616, he made a will, leaving token bequests to Burbage, Heminge, and Condell, but the bulk of his estate to his family. The most famous feature of the will, the bequest of the second-best bed to his wife, reveals nothing about Shakespeare's marriage; the quaintness of the provision seems commonplace to those familiar with ancient testaments. Shakespeare died April 23, 1616, and was buried in the Stratford church where he had been christened. Within seven years a monument was erected to his memory on the north wall of the chancel. Its portrait bust and the Droeshout engraving on the title page of the First Folio provide the only likenesses with an established claim to authenticity. The best verbal vignette was written by his rival Ben Jonson, the more impressive for being imbedded in a context mainly critical :

... I loved the man, and doe honour his memory (on this side idolatry) as much as any. Hee was indeed honest, and of an open and free nature: had an excellent Phantsie, brave notions, and gentle expressions.... (*Timber or Discoveries*, ca. 1623–30)

*

The reader of Shakespeare's plays is aided by a general knowledge of the way in which they were staged. The King's men acquired a roofed and artificially lighted theatre only toward the close of Shakespeare's career, and then only for winter use. Nearly all his plays were designed for performance in such structures as the Globe – a three-tiered amphitheatre with a large rectangular platform extending to the center of its yard. The plays were staged by daylight, by large casts brilliantly costumed, but with only a minimum of properties, without scenery, and quite possibly without intermissions. There was a rear stage gallery for action "above," and a curtained rear recess for "discoveries" and other special effects, but by far the major portion of any play was enacted upon the projecting platform, with episode following episode in swift succession, and with shifts of time and place signaled the audience only by the momentary clearing of the stage between the episodes. Information about the identity of the characters and, when necessary, about the time and place of the action was incorporated in the dialogue. No place-headings have been inserted in the present editions; these are apt to obscure the original fluidity of structure, with the emphasis upon action and speech rather than scenic background. (Indications of place are supplied in the footnotes.) The acting, including that of the youthful apprentices to the profession who performed the parts of women, was highly skillful, with a premium placed upon grace of gesture and beauty of diction. The audiences, a cross section of the general public, commonly numbered a thousand, sometimes more than two thousand. Judged by the type of plays they applauded, these audiences were not only large but also perceptive.

## THE TEXTS OF THE PLAYS

About half of Shakespeare's plays appeared in print for the first time in the folio volume of 1623. The others had been published individually, usually in quarto volumes, during his lifetime or in the six years following his death. The copy used by the printers of the quartos varied greatly in merit, sometimes representing Shakespeare's true text, sometimes only a debased version of that text. The copy used by the printers of the folio also varied in merit, but was chosen with care. Since it consisted of the best available manuscripts, or the more acceptable quartos (although frequently in editions other than the first), or of quartos corrected by reference to manuscripts, we have good or reasonably good texts of most of the thirty-seven plays.

In the present series, the plays have been newly edited from quarto or folio texts, depending, when a choice offered, upon which is now regarded by bibliographical specialists as the more authoritative. The ideal has been to reproduce the chosen texts with as few alterations as possible, beyond occasional relineation, expansion of abbreviations, and modernization of punctuation and spelling. Emendation is held to a minimum, and such material as has been added, in the way of stage directions and lines supplied by an alternative text, has been enclosed in square brackets.

None of the plays printed in Shakespeare's lifetime were divided into acts and scenes, and the inference is that the author's own manuscripts were not so divided. In the folio collection, some of the plays remained undivided, some were divided into acts, and some were divided into acts and scenes. During the eighteenth century all of the plays were divided into acts and scenes, and in the Cambridge edition of the mid-nineteenth century, from which the influential Globe text derived, this division was more or less regularized and the lines were numbered. Many useful works of reference employ the act–scene–line apparatus thus established.

Since this act–scene division is obviously convenient, but is of very dubious authority so far as Shakespeare's own structural principles are concerned, or the original manner of staging his plays, a problem is presented to modern editors. In the present series the act–scene division is retained marginally, and may be viewed as a reference aid like the line numbering. A star marks the points of division when these points have been determined by a cleared stage indicating a shift of time and place in the action of the play, or when no harm results from the editorial assumption that there is such a shift. However, at those points where the established division is clearly misleading – that is, where continuous action has been split up into separate "scenes" – the star is omitted and the distortion corrected. This mechanical expedient seemed the best means of combining utility and accuracy.

THE GENERAL EDITOR

# INTRODUCTION

For the story presented in *The Winter's Tale* no more appropriate title could have been chosen. It is a story such as might have been often told to while away a winter's evening, a story to be heard and reheard with ever increasing pleasure, its very improbabilities and even its geographical and historical inaccuracies being not, as often assumed, the defects of carelessness, but charming if not essential characteristics of an old folk-tale. It is a story of early sadness but of final joy, a story to send the hearers off to bed content with their lot and more tolerant of their fellow-men.

Surviving records attest to a performance at the Globe Theatre witnessed by a Dr Simon Forman on May 15, 1611, and to a presentation at court some six months later. Though the evidence supplied by these records is alone too indecisive to establish the date of composition as 1610–1611, it is strongly supported by evidence within the play itself. In both theme and tone, both diction and verse, *The Winter's Tale* bears the closest resemblance to *Cymbeline* and *The Tempest*. Like them it treats the theme of alienation and reconciliation, destruction and rebirth, and like them it embraces the improbabilities of romance. The language, elliptical, involved, and crammed with thought, is that of Shakespeare's latest manner; as is also the verse, with no rhyme save in the songs and the chorus to Act IV, with many speeches beginning or ending in the middle of the line, and with a higher percentage than has any other play of lines with weak or unstressed endings.

As was his usual practice, Shakespeare in *The Winter's Tale* chose for dramatization a story which had already demonstrated its wide appeal. His source was *Pandosto: The Triumph of Time*, written in 1588 by Robert Greene, whose deathbed attack upon him in 1592 as one "beautified with our feathers" Shakespeare seems to have calmly ignored. Inasmuch as Greene's euphuistic romance was one of the most widely read stories of the day, it could hardly have been to disguise his use of it that Shakespeare changed the names of all the characters or transferred to Sicilia the action Greene had placed in Bohemia and to Bohemia what Greene had assigned to Sicilia. In general Shakespeare follows Greene's narrative quite closely through the first three acts, although both by presenting only the last day of Polixenes' visit and by freeing Hermione of the imprudent behavior of her prototype he discards the obvious motivation of Leontes' jealousy. In Greene the newborn princess is by the king's order entrusted to destiny in a boat without rudder or sail and is by fortunate winds borne to the coast where she is discovered by the Shepherd; none corresponding to Antigonus is present to be devoured by a bear. Most of the other changes Shakespeare introduces prepare for the radical change he was to make in Act V. He has the king upon his own initiative, rather than upon the queen's entreaty, seek the verdict of Apollo's oracle, thereby presenting Leontes somewhat more sympathetically; and he introduces Paulina to torture the jealous king and to convince us of his sincere repentance. That engaging rogue Autolycus is, as is also the Shepherd's clownish son, wholly Shakespeare's. Indeed, for the greater part of Act IV Greene's narrative is but the starting point for Shakespeare's creative imagination. For the happy "snapper-up of unconsidered trifles" *Pandosto* offers only Capnio, a colorless attendant upon the prince, who provides no comedy and serves only to make ready the ship for the lovers' escape from Bohemia and to force the old Shepherd aboard with the telltale jewels. For the prince's wooing of the supposed shepherdess, related by Greene in his characteristic imitation of current pseudo-Arcadian pastoralism and in the language of *Euphues*, Shakespeare substitutes the delightful sheep-shearing in IV, iv, with its true and charming presentation of rural life, for which he is indebted to Greene for nothing beyond the mention of "a meeting of all the farmers' daughters," held before the prince had spied the supposed shepherdess, at which the whole day was spent "in such homely pastimes as shepherds use." For little, indeed, is Shakespeare indebted in this most beautiful and memorable scene; Polixenes' prototype does not learn of his son's love for the unrecognized princess until they have fled across the sea. In Act V Shakespeare completely changes both the denouement and the emphasis. In Greene, Bellaria (Hermione) is not revivified; Pandosto (Leontes), having thrown Dorastus (Florizel) into prison, conceives a lustful passion for his unrecognized daughter Fawnia (Perdita), and after her identity has been established and the marriage of the lovers celebrated, he is driven to suicide by the recollection that he had betrayed his friend Egistus (Polixenes), brought death to his queen and his son Garinter (Mamillius), and incestuously desired his own daughter.

*The Winter's Tale* enjoyed considerable popularity during the years following the May 1611 performance witnessed by Dr Forman. Not only was it acted at court in November of that year, but eighteen months later it was chosen as one of fourteen plays to be presented as part of the festivities honoring the marriage of Princess Elizabeth to the Elector Palatine. Two later court performances are recorded before King James' death, and the play was declared "liked" when presented before King Charles in January 1634. But *The Winter's Tale* hardly suited the taste of the Restoration or the eighteenth century. The next recorded performance was more than a century later – in 1741. It was perhaps this short but not unsuccessful revival which led to there being written within the following fifteen years no fewer than three alterations which sought to adapt the play to the taste of the eighteenth century. The most successful of the three was that by David Garrick, whose *Florizel and Perdita : A Dramatic Pastoral* replaced Shakespeare's as the stage version throughout the remainder of the century. In it the events of sixteen years before are narrated by Camillo to a lord of Bohemia, where all the scenes are laid ; there Paulina with the secreted Hermione has found refuge, and there Leontes, at last repentant, comes to ask forgiveness of Polixenes. By these changes Garrick sought to avoid the transfer of action from Sicilia to Bohemia and back to Sicilia, the lapse of sixteen years between Acts III and IV, and perhaps the absence from the stage for extended periods of certain principal characters. Although Shakespeare's text regained the stage with the opening of the nineteenth century, much of the later criticism of the play may suggest that critics have found it difficult wholly to escape the prejudices inherited from the eighteenth century, for it is only within the past few decades that any have declared *The Winter's Tale* one of Shakespeare's masterpieces.

Although earlier critics recognized in *The Winter's Tale* "the golden glow of Shakespeare's genius," praised the beauty and the force of many of its speeches, and marvelled at the daring mastery of its verse, perhaps most before the 1930's found as much to lament as they did to praise. Naturally comparing the plays of his last period with the great tragedies which preceded them, they thought they recognized a decline in Shakespeare's seriousness of purpose, a lessened interest as well in dramatic technique as in the portrayal of properly motivated characters in understandable human situations ; and to explain the change they offered such suggestions as boredom or exhaustion resulting from prolonged mental strain, or eagerness to capitalize upon the popularity recently achieved by the romantic tragicomedies of Beaumont and Fletcher. They saw in *The Winter's Tale* the characteristic fault of Beaumont and Fletcher, an undue emphasis upon the highly dramatic situation even when it could be secured only by the sacrifice of character and probability. Distressed by the lapse of sixteen years between Acts III and IV, and perhaps ignoring Shakespeare's usual disregard of the unity of time, they declared *The Winter's Tale* a structural failure, an unsuccessful experiment toward the satisfactory structure of dramatized romance achieved only in *The Tempest*.

Most of those who have discussed the play in the past thirty years have seen it in a quite different light. They have reminded us that to the English Renaissance the pastoral was not escape literature, something to be read for entertainment alone, but that, as witnessed by Sir Philip Sidney's *Arcadia*, the intelligent reader was expected to discover there notable images of virtues to be imitated and vices to be shunned. When, therefore, for the plays which closed his career Shakespeare chose to use the material of romance, there is hardly reason to suspect him of being less serious; rather the very improbability and naiveté of the plots should encourage one to expect a serious purpose. The apparent crudity of the dramatic technique – such as the introduction of Father Time to announce the passing of sixteen years, the frequent speeches of Autolycus addressed directly to the audience, the famous exit of Antigonus "pursued by a bear" – should be viewed not as evidence that Shakespeare had become tired or bored or indifferent, but rather as a deliberate and skillful adoption of a technique which, because it was antique and outmoded, artistically became the dramatization of a remote and marvellous tale.

Far from seeking an explanation for an odd decline in

Shakespeare's serious purpose, most recent writers on *The Winter's Tale* have accepted Dr E. M. W. Tillyard's view that the plays of Shakespeare's last period represent a natural development of the interests shown in his tragedies. The full tragic pattern presents three stages – prosperity, destruction, re-creation. Although the emphasis in Shakespeare's tragedies is naturally upon the first two, in most of them there is at the end at least the promise of a new order. In the tragicomedies of his last years his concern is with the final phase of the tragic pattern, Dr Tillyard thought; in them "the old order is destroyed as thoroughly as in the main group of tragedies, and it is this destruction that altogether separates them from the realm of comedy in general and from Shakespeare's own earlier comedies in particular." While in *The Tempest* emphasis is upon the third stage of the pattern, re-creation, the earlier stages being presented only in retrospect, in *The Winter's Tale* Shakespeare presents the full pattern; after giving a brief glimpse of earlier prosperity and happiness, he presents, with almost equal emphasis, complete destruction and happy re-creation. In it we are to recognize, also, the cycle of the seasons, Perdita identified as Spring, and perhaps the theme of the vegetation myth of Proserpina, which Shakespeare underscores by several references. When Proserpina was abducted from her mother Ceres by Pluto, the earth withered and vegetation ceased; only upon her release from the nether world did her mother's spirits revive and fertility return to the earth.

As spring may follow fall only after the intervention of winter, so can rebirth follow destruction only after a period of gestation, and forgiveness follow sin only after proved and continuing repentance. A complete treatment of the tragic pattern demands, therefore, an extended period. The lapse of sixteen years between the first three acts of *The Winter's Tale*, sin, alienation, destruction, and the last two acts, forgiveness, reconciliation, rebirth, though it may be thought awkward dramatically, is essential to a complete treatment of the theme. *The Tempest*, with attention centered upon the last stage of the pattern, and that presented in a single day, may appear more compact, more unified, and in its avoidance of suffering more in the spirit of comedy, but to the same extent it is farther removed from the great tragedies and is, perhaps, less serious, less moral than is *The Winter's Tale* with its insistence that sin be paid for before it be forgiven. This insistence, however, in no way lessens the happiness in which the play ends. No play by Shakespeare has a happier ending, nor can a happier ending be conceived, for the happiness is earned by the characters, not merely decreed by the poet. Leontes, purified by his suffering, a sinner no more, deserves those greatest of joys, forgiveness and reunion with those he loved. Hermione, by her selfless surrender to the dictate of the oracle, has earned not only her restoration but the return of her long-lost daughter. And the lost one, Perdita, surely one of Shakespeare's most charming characters, of royal blood but of country rearing, because of her natural manners and simple honesty merits her happy future with the adoring Florizel.

As Dr Simon Forman in his account of the performance of May 1611 makes no mention of the statue scene, it has been thought by some that this happiest of endings represents a later alteration, that in Shakespeare's original version Hermione, like her prototype in Greene, actually died as reported in Act III, and that the final scene at first presented what is now only related, the identification of Perdita. Forman, however, is here, as always, an unsatisfactory reporter; stating only that the queen was by the oracle declared guiltless, he records nothing of either her death or her supposed death. But whether or not the statue scene be a later addition, it is certainly written by Shakespeare throughout and constitutes the proper – one may almost say the necessary – ending, for the return of

Hermione not only completes the happiness with which
the play ends but, by more closely joining its two parts,
gives to the play a unity it would otherwise lack.

*University of Iowa*           BALDWIN MAXWELL

## NOTE ON THE TEXT

The only text of *The Winter's Tale* is that of the folio of 1623. It
is an excellent text, obviously prepared from clearly written copy.
This copy is now believed to have been a transcript made by the
scrivener Ralph Crane, perhaps from Shakespeare's own draft. A
characteristic of the folio text is the almost complete absence of
stage directions and, save in a few instances, the listing at the
opening of each scene of all the characters who appear during the
scene, generally with no indication of the exact point at which
they enter. In the present text, the entries have been split and
distributed to what appear to be the proper points. The act–scene
division supplied marginally is identical, in the case of this play,
with that of the folio.

Except for a few corrections of obvious typographical errors,
all departures from the folio text are listed below, with the adopted
reading in italics followed by the folio reading in roman. Most
of the alterations first appeared in the later folios or in early
eighteenth-century editions.

*The Names of the Actors* (printed at the end of the play in F)
I, i, 25 *have* hath
I, ii, 124 *heifer* Heycfer   148 *What . . . brother?* (assigned to
Leontes in F)   158 *do* do's   207 *you, they say* you say   231 *th'
entreaties* the Entreaties   253 *forth. In* forth in   275 *hobby-
horse* Holy-Horse   315 *gallèd* gall'd   375–76 *not | Be . . . me?
'Tis* not? | Be . . . me, 'tis   407 *followed* followèd   443 *con-
demnèd* condemnd   460 *off hence.* off, hence:
II, i, 32 s.d. (appears before l. 1 in F)   35 *eyed* eyèd   104 *afar off*
a farre-off
II, ii, 4 s.d. (appears before l. 1 in F)   49 *hammered* hammerèd
53 *let't* le't

II, iii, 4 *th' adulteress* th' Adultresse    26 s.d. (appears before l. 1
in F)    39 *What* Who    60 *good, so* good so

III, ii, 10 *Silence!* (appears as s.d. in F)    s.d. (appears before l. 1
in F)    32 *Who* Whom    122 s.d. (appears before l. 1 in F)
235–36 *unto | Our . . . perpetual. Once* (unto | Our shame per-
petuall) once

III, iii, 48 *begins. Poor* beginnes, poore    57 s.d. *Shepherd* (appears before l. 1 in F)    75 s.d. (appears before l. 1 in F)    112
*made* mad

IV, ii, 52 s.d. *Exeunt* Exit

IV, iii, 7 *on* an    10 *With . . . thrush* With heigh, the Thrush    37
*currants* currence    54 *offends* offend

IV, iv, s.d. (Autolycus enters here in F)    2 *Do* Do's    12 *Digest
it* Digest    13 *swoon* sworne    23 *borrowed* borrowèd    40 *dearest* deer'st    54 s.d. (appears before l. 1 in F)    98 *your* you
105 *wi' th'* with'    242 *kiln-hole* kill-hole    *off* of    292 *Get . . .
go* (not assigned in F)    354 *who* whom    412 *acknowledged*
acknowledge    416 *who* whom    460 *your* my    482 *gleaned*
gleanèd    483 *hide* hides    493 *our* her    516–18 *direction. | If
. . . project | May . . . alteration, on* direction, | If . . . project |
May . . . alteration. On    535–36 *follows: if . . . purpose | But . . .
flight, make* followes, if . . . purpose | But . . . flight; make    542
*the son* there Sonne    658 s.d. *Exeunt* Exit    723 *or toaze* at
toaze    732 *pheasant, cock* Pheazant Cock    824 s.d. *Exit* Exeunt

V, i, 6 *Whilst* Whilest    12 *True* (assigned to Leontes in F)    59
(*Where . . . now*) *appear* soul-vext (Where . . . now appeare)
Soule-vext    61 *just cause* just such cause    75 *I have done*
(assigned to Cleomenes in F)    122 s.d. *Florizel, Perdita* (appears
before l. 1 in F)    159 *his, parting* his parting    168 *whilst*
whilest

V, ii, 20 *haply* happily    61 *This* I his    67 *Wrecked* Wrackt
107 s.d. *Exeunt* Exit

V, iii, 20 s.d. (*Hermione like a statue* appears before l. 1 in F;
Paulina has no s.d. here in F)    67 *fixture* fixure    96 *Or* On

# THE WINTER'S TALE

# THE NAMES OF THE ACTORS

Leontes, *King of Sicilia*
Mamillius, *young Prince of Sicilia*
Camillo
Antigonus
Cleomenes } *four lords of Sicilia*
Dion
Polixenes, *King of Bohemia*
Florizel, *Prince of Bohemia*
Archidamus, *a lord of Bohemia*
Old Shepherd, *reputed father of Perdita*
Clown, *his son*
Autolycus, *a rogue*
[*A Mariner*]
[*A Gaoler*]
Hermione, *Queen to Leontes*
Perdita, *daughter to Leontes and Hermione*
Paulina, *wife to Antigonus*
Emilia, *a lady* [*attending on Hermione*]
[Mopsa
[Dorcas } *shepherdesses*]
Other Lords and Gentlemen, [*Ladies, Officers, and*]
  *Servants, Shepherds, and Shepherdesses*
[*Time, as Chorus*]

[Scene : *Sicilia and Bohemia*]

*Enter Camillo and Archidamus.*                     I, i

ARCHIDAMUS If you shall chance, Camillo, to visit Bohemia on the like occasion whereon my services are now on foot, you shall see, as I have said, great difference betwixt our Bohemia and your Sicilia.

CAMILLO I think this coming summer the King of Sicilia means to pay Bohemia the visitation which he justly owes him.

ARCHIDAMUS Wherein our entertainment shall shame 8 us, we will be justified in our loves; for indeed –

CAMILLO Beseech you –

ARCHIDAMUS Verily, I speak it in the freedom of my knowledge. We cannot with such magnificence – in so rare – I know not what to say. We will give you sleepy drinks, that your senses, unintelligent of our insufficience, may, though they cannot praise us, as little accuse us.

CAMILLO You pay a great deal too dear for what's given freely.

ARCHIDAMUS Believe me, I speak as my understanding instructs me and as mine honesty puts it to utterance.

CAMILLO Sicilia cannot show himself over-kind to Bohemia. They were trained together in their childhoods, and

---

I, i In or near the palace of the King of Sicilia   8–9 (Compare the broken sentences in Archidamus' next speech. He wishes to say here that the love which Polixenes bears Leontes will make up for Bohemia's inability to equal the magnificent entertainment shown Polixenes in Sicilia.)

there rooted betwixt them then such an affection which
23  cannot choose but branch now. Since their more mature
dignities and royal necessities made separation of their
society, their encounters, though not personal, have
26  been royally attorneyed with interchange of gifts, let-
27  ters, loving embassies; that they have seemed to be together, though absent; shook hands, as over a vast; and
embraced, as it were, from the ends of opposed winds.
The heavens continue their loves!

ARCHIDAMUS I think there is not in the world either
malice or matter to alter it. You have an unspeakable
comfort of your young prince Mamillius. It is a gentleman of the greatest promise that ever came into my
note.

CAMILLO I very well agree with you in the hopes of him.
36  It is a gallant child – one that indeed physics the subject, makes old hearts fresh. They that went on crutches
ere he was born desire yet their life to see him a man.

ARCHIDAMUS Would they else be content to die?

CAMILLO Yes – if there were no other excuse why they
should desire to live.

ARCHIDAMUS If the king had no son, they would desire
to live on crutches till he had one.          *Exeunt.*

*

I, ii          *Enter Leontes, Hermione, Mamillius, Polixenes,*
              *Camillo, Lords.*

POLIXENES
1   Nine changes of the wat'ry star hath been
2   The shepherd's note since we have left our throne
    Without a burthen. Time as long again
    Would be filled up, my brother, with our thanks,
    And yet we should, for perpetuity,

23 *branch* flourish   26 *attorneyed* performed by proxy   27 *that* so that
36 *physics* cures (presumably of melancholy)
I, ii The same   1 *wat'ry star* moon   2 *note* observation

Go hence in debt. And therefore, like a cipher,
Yet standing in rich place, I multiply
With one 'We thank you' many thousands moe               8
That go before it.

LEONTES          Stay your thanks a while
And pay them when you part.

POLIXENES               Sir, that's to-morrow.
I am questioned by my fears of what may chance          11
Or breed upon our absence, that may blow
No sneaping winds at home to make us say,               13
'This is put forth too truly.' Besides, I have stayed
To tire your royalty.

LEONTES          We are tougher, brother,
Than you can put us to't.

POLIXENES               No longer stay.

LEONTES
One sev'n-night longer.

POLIXENES               Very sooth, to-morrow.

LEONTES
We'll part the time between's then, and in that
I'll no gainsaying.

POLIXENES          Press me not, beseech you, so.
There is no tongue that moves, none, none i' th' world,
So soon as yours could win me. So it should now
Were there necessity in your request, although
'Twere needful I denied it. My affairs
Do even drag me homeward, which to hinder
Were in your love a whip to me, my stay                 25
To you a charge and trouble. To save both,
Farewell, our brother.

LEONTES          Tongue-tied our queen? Speak you.

HERMIONE
I had thought, sir, to have held my peace until

---

8 *moe* more (Modern English 'more' has absorbed both Early English 'ma':
greater in number, and E.E. 'mara': greater in degree)   11–14 (a difficult
passage; *that may blow* may express a wish or perhaps a purpose, that there
may blow)   13 *sneaping* biting   25 *in* i.e. to make

You had drawn oaths from him not to stay. You, sir,
Charge him too coldly. Tell him you are sure
All in Bohemia's well; this satisfaction
The by-gone day proclaimed. Say this to him,

33    He's beat from his best ward.

LEONTES                              Well said, Hermione.

HERMIONE
To tell he longs to see his son were strong.
But let him say so then, and let him go;
But let him swear so, and he shall not stay,
We'll thwack him hence with distaffs.
Yet of your royal presence I'll adventure
The borrow of a week. When at Bohemia
You take my lord, I'll give him my commission

41    To let him there a month behind the gest
42    Prefixed for's parting. Yet, good deed, Leontes,
43    I love thee not a jar o' th' clock behind
44    What lady she her lord. You'll stay?

POLIXENES                            No, madam.

HERMIONE
Nay, but you will?

POLIXENES            I may not, verily.

HERMIONE
Verily?

47    You put me off with limber vows, but I,
Though you would seek t' unsphere the stars with oaths,
Should yet say, 'Sir, no going.' Verily,
You shall not go. A lady's 'Verily' is
As potent as a lord's. Will you go yet?
Force me to keep you as a prisoner,

53    Not like a guest, so you shall pay your fees
When you depart and save your thanks. How say you?

33 *ward* defense   41 *let him* let him remain; *gest* place and time of a visit
42 *good deed* indeed   43 *jar* tick   44 *What lady she* any lady   47 *limber*
feeble   53 *fees* payments which gaolers usually demanded of prisoners
upon their release

My prisoner or my guest? By your dread 'Verily,'
One of them you shall be.
POLIXENES                    Your guest, then, madam.
To be your prisoner should import offending,                    57
Which is for me less easy to commit
Than you to punish.
HERMIONE                    Not your gaoler, then,
But your kind hostess. Come, I'll question you
Of my lord's tricks and yours when you were boys.
You were pretty lordings then?
POLIXENES                              We were, fair queen,
Two lads that thought there was no more behind
But such a day to-morrow as to-day,
And to be boy eternal.
HERMIONE                    Was not my lord
The verier wag o' th' two?
POLIXENES
We were as twinned lambs that did frisk i' th' sun,
And bleat the one at th' other. What we changed                    68
Was innocence for innocence; we knew not
The doctrine of ill-doing, nor dreamed
That any did. Had we pursued that life,
And our weak spirits ne'er been higher reared
With stronger blood, we should have answered heaven
Boldly 'Not guilty,' the imposition cleared                    74
Hereditary ours.
HERMIONE                    By this we gather
You have tripped since.
POLIXENES                    O my most sacred lady,
Temptations have since then been born to's, for
In those unfledged days was my wife a girl;
Your precious self had then not crossed the eyes
Of my young playfellow.
HERMIONE                    Grace to boot!                    80

---

57 *import offending* i.e. imply that I had committed an offense   68 *changed*
exchanged   74–75 *the imposition . . . ours* freed even from original sin   80
*Grace to boot* Heaven help me

Of this make no conclusion, lest you say
Your queen and I are devils. Yet go on.
Th' offenses we have made you do we'll answer,
If you first sinned with us and that with us
    You did continue fault and that you slipped not
With any but with us.

LEONTES                    Is he won yet?

HERMIONE
He'll stay, my lord.

LEONTES                At my request he would not.
Hermione, my dearest, thou never spok'st
To better purpose.

HERMIONE            Never?

LEONTES                        Never but once.

HERMIONE
What? Have I twice said well? When was't before?
I prithee tell me. Cram 's with praise, and make 's
92    As fat as tame things. One good deed dying tongueless
Slaughters a thousand waiting upon that.
Our praises are our wages. You may ride 's
With one soft kiss a thousand furlongs ere
96    With spur we heat an acre. But to the goal.
My last good deed was to entreat his stay.
What was my first? It has an elder sister,
Or I mistake you. O, would her name were Grace!
But once before I spoke to the purpose. When?
Nay, let me have't; I long.

LEONTES                          Why, that was when
102    Three crabbèd months had soured themselves to death
Ere I could make thee open thy white hand
104    And clap thyself my love. Then didst thou utter
'I am yours for ever.'

HERMIONE            'Tis Grace indeed.

92–93 One . . . that withholding praise of one good deed discourages a
thousand others   96 heat race; to the goal to come to the point   102
crabbèd bitter   104 clap pledge

Why, lo you now, I have spoke to the purpose twice;
The one for ever earned a royal husband,
Th' other for some while a friend.
    *[Gives her hand to Polixenes, and they walk apart.]*
LEONTES *[aside]*              Too hot, too hot!
To mingle friendship far is mingling bloods.
I have tremor cordis on me. My heart dances,
But not for joy, not joy. This entertainment                    111
May a free face put on, derive a liberty
From heartiness, from bounty, fertile bosom,
And well become the agent. 'T may, I grant.
But to be paddling palms and pinching fingers,                    115
As now they are, and making practiced smiles
As in a looking-glass, and then to sigh, as 'twere
The mort o' th' deer – O, that is entertainment                    118
My bosom likes not, nor my brows. Mamillius,
Art thou my boy?
MAMILLIUS         Ay, my good lord.
LEONTES                   I' fecks!                    120
Why, that's my bawcock. What, hast smutched thy nose?                    121
They say it is a copy out of mine. Come, captain,
We must be neat – not neat but cleanly, captain.
And yet the steer, the heifer, and the calf
Are all called neat. – Still virginalling                    125
Upon his palm? – How now, you wanton calf?
Art thou my calf?
MAMILLIUS        Yes, if you will, my lord.
LEONTES
Thou want'st a rough pash and the shoots that I have,                    128
To be full like me; yet they say we are
Almost as like as eggs. Women say so,

---

111-14 *This . . . agent* Hermione's gracious entertainment may well become
her if it be due to a hospitable and generous nature  115 *paddling* caressing
118 *mort o' th' deer* hunter's horn announcing the death of the deer  120
*I' fecks* in faith  121 *bawcock* fine fellow (Fr. 'beau coq'); *smutched* smudged
125 *neat* (1) cleanly, (2) horned cattle; *virginalling* playing (with fingers)
128 *pash . . . shoots* head . . . horns

That will say anything. But were they false
13　As o'er-dyed blacks, as wind, as waters, false
As dice are to be wished by one that fixes
No bourn 'twixt his and mine, yet were it true
To say this boy were like me. Come, sir page,
136　Look on me with your welkin eye. Sweet villain!
137　Most dear'st! my collop! Can thy dam? – may't be? –
138　Affection, thy intention stabs the center!
Thou dost make possible things not so held,
Communicat'st with dreams – how can this be?
With what's unreal thou coactive art,
And fellow'st nothing. Then 'tis very credent
Thou may'st co-join with something; and thou dost,
And that beyond commission, and I find it,
And that to the infection of my brains
And hard'ning of my brows.

POLIXENES　　　　　　　　What means Sicilia?

HERMIONE
He something seems unsettled.

POLIXENES　　　　　　　　How, my lord?
148　What cheer? How is't with you, best brother?

HERMIONE　　　　　　　　　　　　　You look
As if you held a brow of much distraction.
Are you moved, my lord?

LEONTES　　　　　　　　No, in good earnest.
How sometimes nature will betray its folly,
Its tenderness, and make itself a pastime
To harder bosoms! Looking on the lines
154　Of my boy's face, methoughts I did recoil
Twenty-three years, and saw myself unbreeched,

---

**132** *o'er-dyed blacks* colored fabrics dyed black or weakened by too much dyeing　**136** *welkin* sky-blue　**137** *collop* small portion　**137–46** *Can . . . brows* (the incoherency of this passage reflects Leontes' tortured mind)　**138** *intention* intensity　**148** *What cheer . . . brother* (Though the folio gives these words to Leontes, most editors assign them to Polixenes. Spoken by Leontes, they may suggest a forced gaiety.)　**154** *methoughts* it seemed to me (variant of 'methought')

In my green velvet coat, my dagger muzzled
Lest it should bite its master and so prove,
As ornaments oft do, too dangerous.
How like, methought, I then was to this kernel,
This squash, this gentleman. Mine honest friend,
Will you take eggs for money?                        161

MAMILLIUS                    No, my lord, I'll fight.

LEONTES
You will? Why, happy man be's dole! My brother,    162
Are you so fond of your young prince as we
Do seem to be of ours?

POLIXENES                    If at home, sir,
He's all my exercise, my mirth, my matter,
Now my sworn friend and then mine enemy,
My parasite, my soldier, statesman, all.
He makes a July's day short as December,
And with his varying childness cures in me
Thoughts that would thick my blood.                  170

LEONTES                              So stands this squire
Officed with me. We two will walk, my lord,
And leave you to your graver steps. Hermione,
How thou lov'st us, show in our brother's welcome.
Let what is dear in Sicily be cheap.
Next to thyself and my young rover, he's
Apparent to my heart.                                176

HERMIONE                    If you would seek us,
We are yours i' th' garden. Shall's attend you there?

LEONTES
To your own bents dispose you. You'll be found,
Be you beneath the sky. *[aside]* I am angling now,
Though you perceive me not how I give line.
Go to, go to!
How she holds up the neb, the bill to him,            182
And arms her with the boldness of a wife

---

161 *take . . . money* be imposed upon   162 *dole* lot   170 *thick my blood*
make me melancholy   176 *Apparent* heir apparent   182 *neb* face

184 To her allowing husband!
    *[Exeunt Polixenes, Hermione, and Attendants.]*
     Gone already!
185 Inch-thick, knee-deep, o'er head and ears a forked one!
 Go play, boy, play. Thy mother plays, and I
187 Play too, but so disgraced a part, whose issue
 Will hiss me to my grave. Contempt and clamor
 Will be my knell. Go play, boy, play. There have been,
 Or I am much deceived, cuckolds ere now;
 And many a man there is, even at this present,
 Now while I speak this, holds his wife by th' arm,
 That little thinks she has been sluiced in's absence
 And his pond fished by his next neighbor, by
 Sir Smile, his neighbor. Nay, there's comfort in't
 Whiles other men have gates and those gates opened,
 As mine, against their will. Should all despair
 That have revolted wives, the tenth of mankind
 Would hang themselves. Physic for't there's none.
200 It is a bawdy planet, that will strike
 Where 'tis predominant; and 'tis powerful, think it,
 From east, west, north, and south. Be it concluded,
 No barricado for a belly. Know't,
 It will let in and out the enemy
205 With bag and baggage. Many thousand on's
 Have the disease and feel't not. How now, boy?

MAMILLIUS
 I am like you, they say.
LEONTES     Why, that's some comfort.
 What, Camillo there?
CAMILLO
 Ay, my good lord.
LEONTES
 Go play, Mamillius. Thou'rt an honest man.
         *[Exit Mamillius.]*

---

184 *allowing* approving 185 *forked one* horned one (cuckold) 187 *whose issue* the result of which 200–01 *It is . . . predominant* unchastity, like a baneful planet, destroys when in ascendant 205 *on's* of us

Camillo, this great sir will yet stay longer.

CAMILLO
You had much ado to make his anchor hold;
When you cast out, it still came home. 213

LEONTES Didst note it?

CAMILLO
He would not stay at your petitions, made
His business more material

LEONTES Didst perceive it?

    *[Aside]*
They're here with me already, whisp'ring, rounding 216
'Sicilia is a so-forth.' 'Tis far gone,
When I shall gust it last. How came't, Camillo, 218
That he did stay?

CAMILLO At the good queen's entreaty.

LEONTES
At the queen's be't. 'Good' should be pertinent;
But so it is, it is not. Was this taken 221
By any understanding pate but thine?
For thy conceit is soaking, will draw in 223
More than the common blocks. Not noted, is't,
But of the finer natures, by some severals 225
Of head-piece extraordinary? Lower messes 226
Perchance are to this business purblind? Say. 227

CAMILLO
Business, my lord? I think most understand
Bohemia stays here longer.

LEONTES Ha?

CAMILLO Stays here longer.

LEONTES
Ay, but why?

---

**213** *still* always  **216–17** *They're here . . . so-forth* people are already mock-ing me, whispering I am a so-and-so (perhaps Leontes, unable to say 'cuckold,' puts two fingers to his head to suggest horns)  **218** *gust* realize  **221** *so* as; *taken* recognized  **223** *conceit is soaking* understanding is absorb-ing  **225** *severals* individuals  **226** *Lower messes* inferior men (who at table occupy lower seats)  **227** *purblind* wholly blind

CAMILLO
> To satisfy your highness and th' entreaties
> Of our most gracious mistress.

232 LEONTES                              Satisfy
> Th' entreaties of your mistress? Satisfy;
> Let that suffice. I have trusted thee, Camillo,
> With all the nearest things to my heart, as well
> My chamber-councils, wherein, priest-like, thou
> Hast cleansed my bosom, I from thee departed
> Thy penitent reformed. But we have been
> Deceived in thy integrity, deceived
> In that which seems so.

CAMILLO                        Be it forbid, my lord!

LEONTES
241 > To bide upon't, thou art not honest; or,
> If thou inclin'st that way, thou art a coward,
243 > Which hoxes honesty behind, restraining
> From course required; or else thou must be counted
245 > A servant grafted in my serious trust
> And therein negligent; or else a fool
> That seest a game played home, the rich stake drawn,
> And tak'st it all for jest.

CAMILLO                        My gracious lord,
> I may be negligent, foolish, and fearful.
> In every one of these no man is free,
> But that his negligence, his folly, fear,
> Among the infinite doings of the world,
253 > Sometime puts forth. In your affairs, my lord,
> If ever I were willful-negligent,
255 > It was my folly; if industriously
> I played the fool, it was my negligence,
> Not weighing well the end; if ever fearful
> To do a thing where I the issue doubted,
> Whereof the execution did cry out

232 *Satisfy* (Leontes fixes upon the sexual connotation)   241 *bide* dwell
243 *hoxes* disables   245 *grafted . . . trust* insinuated into my confidence
253 *puts forth* reveals itself   255 *industriously* willfully

36

Against the non-performance, 'twas a fear
Which oft infects the wisest. These, my lord,
Are such allowed infirmities that honesty
Is never free of. But, beseech your grace,
Be plainer with me ; let me know my trespass
By its own visage. If I deny it,
'Tis none of mine.

LEONTES                    Ha' not you seen, Camillo –
But that's past doubt, you have, or your eye-glass          267
Is thicker than a cuckold's horn – or heard –              268
For to a vision so apparent rumor
Cannot be mute – or thought – for cogitation
Resides not in that man that does not think –
My wife is slippery ? If thou wilt confess,
Or else be impudently negative,
To have nor eyes nor ears nor thought, then say
My wife 's a hobby-horse, deserves a name
As rank as any flax-wench that puts to
Before her troth-plight. Say 't and justify 't.

CAMILLO
I would not be a stander-by to hear
My sovereign mistress clouded so, without
My present vengeance taken. 'Shrew my heart,          280
You never spoke what did become you less
Than this, which to reiterate were sin                282
As deep as that, though true.

LEONTES                    Is whispering nothing ?
Is leaning cheek to cheek ? Is meeting noses ?
Kissing with inside lip ? stopping the career           285
Of laughter with a sigh ? – a note infallible
Of breaking honesty ! – horsing foot on foot ?          287
Skulking in corners ? wishing clocks more swift ?
Hours, minutes ? noon, midnight ? and all eyes

267 *eye-glass* crystalline lens of the eye  268 *thicker* more opaque  280
*present* immediate; *'Shrew* beshrew, curse  282–83 *which . . . true* to
repeat the charge against her would be a sin as great as her infidelity were
she guilty  285 *career* full gallop  287 *honesty* chastity

290 Blind with the pin and web but theirs, theirs only,
That would unseen be wicked? Is this nothing?
Why, then the world and all that's in't is nothing,
The covering sky is nothing, Bohemia nothing,
My wife is nothing, nor nothing have these nothings,
If this be nothing.

CAMILLO          Good my lord, be cured
296 Of this diseased opinion, and betimes,
For 'tis most dangerous.

LEONTES          Say it be, 'tis true.

CAMILLO
No, no, my lord.

LEONTES          It is. You lie, you lie.
I say thou liest, Camillo, and I hate thee,
Pronounce thee a gross lout, a mindless slave,
301 Or else a hovering temporizer, that
Canst with thine eyes at once see good and evil,
Inclining to them both. Were my wife's liver
Infected as her life, she would not live
305 The running of one glass.

CAMILLO          Who does infect her?

LEONTES
Why, he that wears her like her medal, hanging
About his neck – Bohemia, who, if I
Had servants true about me that bare eyes
To see alike mine honor as their profits,
Their own particular thrifts, they would do that
Which should undo more doing. Ay, and thou,
312 His cupbearer – whom I from meaner form
313 Have benched and reared to worship, who may'st see
Plainly as heaven sees earth and earth sees heaven,
How I am gallèd – might'st bespice a cup
To give mine enemy a lasting wink,
Which draught to me were cordial.

290 *pin and web* cataract  296 *betimes* at once  301 *hovering* irresolute
305 *glass* hourglass  312 *meaner form* humbler position  313 *benched* placed
in authority; *worship* position of honor

CAMILLO                              Sir, my lord,
　I could do this, and that with no rash potion,
　But with a ling'ring dram that should not work
　Maliciously like poison. But I cannot
　Believe this crack to be in my dread mistress,
　So sovereignly being honorable.
　I have loved thee –                                    323
LEONTES              Make that thy question, and go rot!
　Dost think I am so muddy, so unsettled,
　To appoint myself in this vexation, sully
　The purity and whiteness of my sheets –
　Which to preserve is sleep, which being spotted
　Is goads, thorns, nettles, tails of wasps –
　Give scandal to the blood o' th' prince my son,
　Who I do think is mine and love as mine,
　Without ripe moving to't? Would I do this?           331
　Could man so blench?                                  332
CAMILLO                      I must believe you, sir.
　I do, and will fetch off Bohemia for't;
　Provided that, when he's removed, your highness
　Will take again your queen as yours at first,
　Even for your son's sake, and thereby for sealing
　The injury of tongues in courts and kingdoms
　Known and allied to yours.
LEONTES                      Thou dost advise me
　Even so as I mine own course have set down.
　I'll give no blemish to her honor, none.
CAMILLO                              My lord,
　Go then, and with a countenance as clear             341
　As friendship wears at feasts, keep with Bohemia
　And with your queen. I am his cupbearer.
　If from me he have wholesome beverage,
　Account me not your servant.

323 (as Camillo would hardly be expected to use *thee* in addressing his king,
some editors assign the entire line to Leontes)  331 *Without ripe moving*
without good reason (the phrase goes with *appoint, sully, give scandal*)  332
*blench* deceive himself  341 *clear* innocent

LEONTES            This is all.
Do't, and thou hast the one half of my heart;
Do't not, thou split'st thine own.

CAMILLO         I'll do't, my lord.

LEONTES
I will seem friendly, as thou hast advised me.     *Exit.*

CAMILLO
O miserable lady! But for me,
What case stand I in? I must be the poisoner
Of good Polixenes; and my ground to do't
Is the obedience to a master, one
Who in rebellion with himself will have
354   All that are his so too. To do this deed,
Promotion follows. If I could find example
Of thousands that had struck anointed kings
And flourished after, I'ld not do't; but since
Nor brass nor stone nor parchment bears not one,
Let villainy itself forswear't. I must
360   Forsake the court. To do't, or no, is certain
361   To me a break-neck. Happy star reign now!
Here comes Bohemia.
         *Enter Polixenes.*

POLIXENES        This is strange. Methinks
363   My favor here begins to warp. Not speak?
Good day, Camillo.

CAMILLO        Hail, most royal sir!

POLIXENES
What is the news i' th' court?

365 CAMILLO          None rare, my lord.

POLIXENES
The king hath on him such a countenance
As he had lost some province and a region
368   Loved as he loves himself. Even now I met him

---

354 *so too* i.e. in rebellion against (false to) themselves   360 *To do't* to kill Polixenes   361 *Happy star* good fortune   363 *Not speak* (Polixenes refers to Leontes, whom he encountered on his way in)   365 *rare* unusual   368 *met* greeted

With customary compliment, when he,
Wafting his eyes to th' contrary and falling
A lip of much contempt, speeds from me, and
So leaves me to consider what is breeding
That changes thus his manners.

CAMILLO
　I dare not know, my lord.

POLIXENES
　How dare not? do not? Do you know and dare not
　Be intelligent to me? 'Tis thereabouts,                  376
　For, to yourself, what you do know, you must,
　And cannot say you dare not. Good Camillo,
　Your changed complexions are to me a mirror
　Which shows me mine changed too, for I must be
　A party in this alteration, finding
　Myself thus altered with't.

CAMILLO                     There is a sickness
　Which puts some of us in distemper, but
　I cannot name the disease, and it is caught
　Of you that yet are well.

POLIXENES                   How caught of me?
　Make me not sighted like the basilisk.                   386
　I have looked on thousands who have sped the better
　By my regard, but killed none so. Camillo,               388
　As you are certainly a gentleman, thereto
　Clerk-like experienced – which no less adorns            390
　Our gentry than our parents' noble names,
　In whose success we are gentle – I beseech you,          392
　If you know aught which does behove my knowledge
　Thereof to be informed, imprison't not
　In ignorant concealment.

CAMILLO                      I may not answer.

---

376 *intelligent* intelligible; *'Tis thereabouts* it is something of the sort    386
*Make . . . basilisk* attribute not to me a sight like that of the fabulous serpent
whose look or breath was fatal    388 *regard* look    390 *Clerk-like* like a
scholar    392 *In whose success* in succession from whom

POLIXENES
A sickness caught of me, and yet I well?
I must be answered. Dost thou hear, Camillo?
I conjure thee by all the parts of man
Which honor does acknowledge, whereof the least
Is not this suit of mine, that thou declare
401    What incidency thou dost guess of harm
Is creeping toward me; how far off, how near;
Which way to be prevented, if to be;
If not, how best to bear it.

CAMILLO               Sir, I will tell you,
Since I am charged in honor and by him
That I think honorable. Therefore mark my counsel,
Which must be even as swiftly followed as
I mean to utter it, or both yourself and me
409    Cry 'Lost,' and so good night!

POLIXENES          On, good Camillo.

CAMILLO
I am appointed him to murder you.

POLIXENES
By whom, Camillo?

CAMILLO        By the king.

POLIXENES          For what?

CAMILLO
He thinks, nay, with all confidence he swears,
As he had seen't or been an instrument
414    To vice you to't, that you have touched his queen
Forbiddenly.

POLIXENES    O, then my best blood turn
To an infected jelly and my name
Be yoked with his that did betray the Best!
Turn then my freshest reputation to
A savor that may strike the dullest nostril
Where I arrive, and my approach be shunned,

---

401 *incidency* happening   409 *good night* this is the end (as in modern slang, an expression of finality)   414 *vice* force

Nay, hated too, worse than the great'st infection
That e'er was heard or read!
CAMILLO                          Swear his thought over
  By each particular star in heaven and
  By all their influences, you may as well
  Forbid the sea for to obey the moon
  As or by oath remove or counsel shake                    426
  The fabric of his folly, whose foundation                427
  Is piled upon his faith and will continue
  The standing of his body.
POLIXENES                    How should this grow?
CAMILLO
  I know not. But I am sure 'tis safer to
  Avoid what's grown than question how 'tis born.
  If therefore you dare trust my honesty,
  That lies enclosèd in this trunk which you                433
  Shall bear along impawned, away to-night!                434
  Your followers I will whisper to the business,            435
  And will by twos and threes at several posterns           436
  Clear them o' th' city. For myself, I'll put
  My fortunes to your service, which are here
  By this discovery lost. Be not uncertain,
  For, by the honor of my parents, I
  Have uttered truth, which if you seek to prove,
  I dare not stand by; nor shall you be safer
  Than one condemnèd by the king's own mouth,
  Thereon his execution sworn.
POLIXENES                      I do believe thee;
  I saw his heart in's face. Give me thy hand.
  Be pilot to me and thy places shall                      446
  Still neighbor mine. My ships are ready and
  My people did expect my hence departure
  Two days ago. This jealousy

426 *or . . . or* either . . . or   427 *fabric* creation   433 *trunk* body   434 *impawned* as a pledge   435 *whisper to* secretly tell of   436 *posterns* back doors
446–47 *thy places . . . mine* i.e. you may always have an appointment in my household

43

Is for a precious creature. As she's rare,
Must it be great; and as his person's mighty,
Must it be violent; and as he does conceive
He is dishonored by a man which ever
454   Professed to him, why, his revenges must
455   In that be made more bitter. Fear o'ershades me.
456   Good expedition be my friend, and comfort
457   The gracious queen, part of his theme but nothing
Of his ill-ta'en suspicion! Come, Camillo.
I will respect thee as a father if
460   Thou bear'st my life off hence. Let us avoid.

CAMILLO
It is in mine authority to command
The keys of all the posterns. Please your highness
To take the urgent hour. Come, sir, away.     *Exeunt.*

\*

II, i     *Enter Hermione, Mamillius, Ladies.*

HERMIONE
1   Take the boy to you. He so troubles me,
'Tis past enduring.

LADY              Come, my gracious lord,
Shall I be your playfellow?

MAMILLIUS          No, I'll none of you.

LADY
Why, my sweet lord?

MAMILLIUS
You'll kiss me hard and speak to me as if
I were a baby still. I love you better.

SECOND LADY
And why so, my lord?

MAMILLIUS         Not for because

---

454 *Professed* professed love   455 *o'ershades* covers   456 *expedition* prompt
action   457–58 *part . . . suspicion* also object of the king's anger though
innocent of wrongdoing   460 *avoid* depart
II, i In the palace of Leontes   1 *Take . . . to you* take charge of the boy

Your brows are blacker. Yet black brows, they say,
Become some women best, so that there be not
Too much hair there, but in a semicircle,
Or a half-moon made with a pen.

SECOND LADY                        Who taught' this?            11

MAMILLIUS
I learned it out of women's faces. Pray now,
What color are your eyebrows?

LADY                               Blue, my lord.

MAMILLIUS
Nay, that's a mock. I have seen a lady's nose
That has been blue, but not her eyebrows.

LADY                               Hark ye.
The queen your mother rounds apace. We shall
Present our services to a fine new prince
One of these days, and then you'ld wanton with us,      18
If we would have you.

SECOND LADY           She is spread of late
Into a goodly bulk. Good time encounter her!              20

HERMIONE
What wisdom stirs amongst you? Come, sir, now           21
I am for you again. Pray you sit by us
And tell's a tale.

MAMILLIUS       Merry or sad shall't be?

HERMIONE
As merry as you will.

MAMILLIUS
A sad tale's best for winter. I have one
Of sprites and goblins.

HERMIONE           Let's have that, good sir.
Come on, sit down. Come on, and do your best
To fright me with your sprites; you're powerful at it.

MAMILLIUS
There was a man –

HERMIONE           Nay, come sit down; then on.

11 *taught'* taught thee   18 *wanton* play   20 *Gooa time encounter* good fortune attend   21 *wisdom stirs* wise matter is discussed

MAMILLIUS
Dwelt by a churchyard. I will tell it softly ;
31      Yond crickets shall not hear it.

HERMIONE                         Come on, then,
And give't me in mine ear.
          *[Enter] Leontes, Antigonus, Lords [and others].*

LEONTES
Was he met there ? his train ? Camillo with him ?

LORD
Behind the tuft of pines I met them. Never
35      Saw I men scour so on their way. I eyed them
Even to their ships.

LEONTES                    How blest am I
In my just censure, in my true opinion !
38      Alack, for lesser knowledge ! how accursed
In being so blest ! There may be in the cup
A spider steeped, and one may drink, depart,
And yet partake no venom, for his knowledge
Is not infected ; but if one present
Th' abhorred ingredient to his eye, make known
How he hath drunk, he cracks his gorge, his sides,
45      With violent hefts. I have drunk, and seen the spider.
Camillo was his help in this, his pander.
There is a plot against my life, my crown.
All's true that is mistrusted. That false villain
Whom I employed was pre-employed by him.
50      He has discovered my design, and I
51      Remain a pinched thing – yea, a very trick
For them to play at will. How came the posterns
So easily open ?

LORD                    By his great authority,
Which often hath no less prevailed than so
On your command.

31 *crickets* i.e. the 'ladies in waiting with their tittering and chirping laughter' (Furness)   35 *scour* hasten   38 *Alack . . . knowledge* O, that my knowledge were less   45 *hefts* heavings   50 *discovered* revealed   51 *a pinched thing* 'a wretch upon the rack' (Wilson), 'a puppet' (Heath); *trick* toy

46

LEONTES                I know't too well.
Give me the boy. I am glad you did not nurse him.
Though he does bear some signs of me, yet you
Have too much blood in him.

HERMIONE                        What is this? sport?                58

LEONTES
Bear the boy hence. He shall not come about her.
Away with him! and let her sport herself
With that she's big with, for 'tis Polixenes
Has made thee swell thus.

HERMIONE                        But I'ld say he had not,
And I'll be sworn you would believe my saying,
Howe'er you lean to the nayward.                                    64

LEONTES                        You, my lords,
Look on her, mark her well. Be but about
To say 'She is a goodly lady,' and
The justice of your hearts will thereto add
''Tis pity she's not honest, honorable.'
Praise her but for this her without-door form –                    69
Which on my faith deserves high speech – and straight
The shrug, the hum or ha, these petty brands
That calumny doth use – O, I am out,                               72
That mercy does, for calumny will sear
Virtue itself – these shrugs, these hums and ha's,
When you have said she's goodly, come between                      75
Ere you can say she's honest. But be't known,
From him that has most cause to grieve it should be,
She's an adult'ress.

HERMIONE                        Should a villain say so,
The most replenished villain in the world,                         79
He were as much more villain. You, my lord,
Do but mistake.

LEONTES                You have mistook, my lady,
Polixenes for Leontes. O thou thing!

---

**58** *sport* jesting  **64** *nayward* negative  **69** *without-door form* outward
appearance  **72** *out* mistaken  **75** *come between* interfere  **79** *replenished*
full

83    Which I'll not call a creature of thy place,
      Lest barbarism, making me the precedent,
      Should a like language use to all degrees
      And mannerly distinguishment leave out
      Betwixt the prince and beggar. I have said
      She's an adult'ress ; I have said with whom.
      More, she's a traitor and Camillo is
90    A federary with her, and one that knows
      What she should shame to know herself
      But with her most vile principal, that she's
93    A bed-swerver, even as bad as those
94    That vulgars give bold'st titles – ay, and privy
      To this their late escape.

HERMIONE          No, by my life,
      Privy to none of this. How will this grieve you,
      When you shall come to clearer knowledge, that
      You thus have published me ! Gentle my lord,
99    You scarce can right me throughly then to say
      You did mistake.

LEONTES          No. If I mistake
      In those foundations which I build upon,
102   The center is not big enough to bear
      A schoolboy's top. Away with her to prison !
104   He who shall speak for her is afar off guilty
      But that he speaks.

HERMIONE          There's some ill planet reigns.
      I must be patient till the heavens look
      With an aspect more favorable. Good my lords,
      I am not prone to weeping, as our sex
      Commonly are ; the want of which vain dew
      Perchance shall dry your pities. But I have
      That honorable grief lodged here which burns
      Worse than tears drown. Beseech you all, my lords,

---

83 *place* rank   90 *federary* confederate   93 *bed-swerver* adulteress   94
*vulgars . . . titles* common people call rudest names   99 *throughly* thoroughly
102 *center* earth   104–05 *He . . . speaks* he is indirectly guilty who merely
speaks in her behalf

With thoughts so qualified as your charities                         113
Shall best instruct you, measure me; and so                          114
The king's will be performed.

LEONTES                              Shall I be heard?

HERMIONE
Who is't that goes with me? Beseech your highness,
My women may be with me, for you see
My plight requires it. Do not weep, good fools;                      118
There is no cause. When you shall know your mistress
Has deserved prison, then abound in tears
As I come out. This action I now go on
Is for my better grace. Adieu, my lord.
I never wished to see you sorry; now
I trust I shall. My women, come; you have leave.

LEONTES
Go, do our bidding. Hence!
                              *[Exit Queen, guarded, with Ladies.]*

LORD
Beseech your highness, call the queen again.

ANTIGONUS
Be certain what you do, sir, lest your justice
Prove violence, in the which three great ones suffer,                128
Yourself, your queen, your son.

LORD                              For her, my lord,
I dare my life lay down and will do't, sir,
Please you t' accept it, that the queen is spotless
I' th' eyes of heaven and to you – I mean,
In this which you accuse her.

ANTIGONUS                              If it prove
She's otherwise, I'll keep my stables where                          134
I lodge my wife. I'll go in couples with her,
Than when I feel and see her no farther trust her;

---

113 *qualified* modified   114 *measure* judge   118 *fools* (a term of endear-
ment)   128 *violence* outrage   134–35 *I'll . . . her* (perhaps in part the
meaning of this puzzling passage is: 'I'll guard the stables where my wife
lives and never leave her alone' – *stables* intended to suggest a beast to be
ridden)

For every inch of woman in the world,
Ay, every dram of woman's flesh is false,
If she be.

LEONTES   Hold your peaces.

LORD                                     Good my lord –

ANTIGONUS
It is for you we speak, not for ourselves.
You are abused and by some putter-on
That will be damned for't. Would I knew the villain,
143   I would land-damn him. Be she honor-flawed,
I have three daughters – the eldest is eleven,
The second and the third, nine and some five –
If this prove true, they'll pay for't. By mine honor,
I'll geld 'em all; fourteen they shall not see
148   To bring false generations. They are co-heirs,
149   And I had rather glib myself than they
Should not produce fair issue.

LEONTES                        Cease; no more.
You smell this business with a sense as cold
As is a dead man's nose; but I do see't and feel't,
As you feel doing thus [pinches Antigonus], and see withal
154   The instruments that feel.

ANTIGONUS                  If it be so,
We need no grave to bury honesty;
There's not a grain of it the face to sweeten
Of the whole dungy earth.

LEONTES                  What? Lack I credit?

LORD
I had rather you did lack than I, my lord,
159   Upon this ground; and more it would content me
To have her honor true than your suspicion,
Be blamed for't how you might.

LEONTES                        Why, what need we
Commune with you of this, but rather follow

143 *land-damn* (the 'damn' reveals the meaning of this 'mysterious compound') 148 *bring . . . generations* beget bastards 149 *glib* geld 154 *instruments that feel* i.e. Leontes' fingers 159 *ground* matter

Our forceful instigation? Our prerogative                    163
Calls not your counsels, but our natural goodness            164
Imparts this, which if you – or stupified                     165
Or seeming so in skill – cannot or will not                   166
Relish a truth like us, inform yourselves
We need no more of your advice. The matter,
The loss, the gain, the ord'ring on't, is all
Properly ours.

ANTIGONUS      And I wish, my liege,
You had only in your silent judgment tried it,
Without more overture.                                       172

LEONTES                    How could that be?
Either thou art most ignorant by age
Or thou wert born a fool. Camillo's flight,
Added to their familiarity –
Which was as gross as ever touched conjecture,
That lacked sight only, nought for approbation
But only seeing, all other circumstances
Made up to th' deed – doth push on this proceeding.
Yet, for a greater confirmation –
For in an act of this importance 'twere
Most piteous to be wild – I have dispatched in post          182
To sacred Delphos, to Apollo's temple,
Cleomenes and Dion, whom you know
Of stuffed sufficiency. Now from the oracle                  185
They will bring all, whose spiritual counsel had,
Shall stop or spur me. Have I done well?

LORD
Well done, my lord.

LEONTES
Though I am satisfied and need no more
Than what I know, yet shall the oracle
Give rest to th' minds of others, such as he
Whose ignorant credulity will not

163 *instigation* incentive   164 *Calls* calls for   165 *Imparts* bestows
166 *skill* discernment   172 *overture* public revelation   182 *wild* rash;
*post* haste   185 *stuffed sufficiency* full competence

193    Come up to th' truth. So have we thought it good
194    From our free person she should be confined,
Lest that the treachery of the two fled hence
Be left her to perform. Come, follow us.
We are to speak in public, for this business
198    Will raise us all.
ANTIGONUS *[aside]*  To laughter, as I take it,
If the good truth were known.                    *Exeunt.*

\*

II, ii          *Enter Paulina, a Gentleman [and Attendants].*
PAULINA
The keeper of the prison, call to him;
Let him have knowledge who I am.    *[Exit Gentleman.]*
                                    Good lady,
No court in Europe is too good for thee.
What dost thou then in prison?
          *[Enter Gentleman with the] Gaoler.*
                                    Now, good sir,
You know me, do you not?
GAOLER                      For a worthy lady
And one who much I honor.
PAULINA                      Pray you then,
Conduct me to the queen.
GAOLER                      I may not, madam.
To the contrary I have express commandment.
PAULINA
Here's ado,
To lock up honesty and honor from
11    Th' access of gentle visitors. Is't lawful, pray you,
To see her women? any of them? Emilia?
GAOLER
So please you, madam,
To put apart these your attendants, I
Shall bring Emilia forth.

193 *Come up to* face   194 *free* easily accessible   198 *raise* rouse to action
II, ii A prison   11 *lawful* permitted (satirical)

PAULINA            I pray now, call her.
   Withdraw yourselves.
        *[Exeunt Gentleman and Attendants.]*
GAOLER            And, madam,
   I must be present at your conference.
PAULINA
   Well, be't so, prithee.          *[Exit Gaoler.]*
   Here's such ado to make no stain a stain
   As passes coloring.                  20
      *[Enter Gaoler with] Emilia.*
            Dear gentlewoman,
   How fares our gracious lady?
EMILIA
   As well as one so great and so forlorn
   May hold together. On her frights and griefs,
   Which never tender lady hath borne greater,
   She is something before her time delivered.    25
PAULINA
   A boy?
EMILIA    A daughter, and a goodly babe,
   Lusty and like to live. The queen receives
   Much comfort in't, says, 'My poor prisoner,
   I am innocent as you.'
PAULINA          I dare be sworn.
   These dangerous unsafe lunes i' th' king, beshrew them!   30
   He must be told on't, and he shall. The office
   Becomes a woman best; I'll take't upon me.
   If I prove honey-mouthed, let my tongue blister
   And never to my red-looked anger be         34
   The trumpet any more. Pray you, Emilia,
   Commend my best obedience to the queen.
   If she dares trust me with her little babe,
   I'll show't the king and undertake to be
   Her advocate to th' loud'st. We do not know
   How he may soften at the sight o' th' child.

---

20 *passes coloring* surpasses belief    25 *something* somewhat    30 *lunes* fits of
lunacy    34 *red-looked* red-faced

    The silence often of pure innocence
    Persuades when speaking fails.

EMILIA                   Most worthy madam,
    Your honor and your goodness is so evident

44   That your free undertaking cannot miss
    A thriving issue. There is no lady living
    So meet for this great errand. Please your ladyship

47   To visit the next room, I'll presently
    Acquaint the queen of your most noble offer,

49   Who but to-day hammered of this design,

50   But durst not tempt a minister of honor
    Lest she should be denied.

PAULINA             Tell her, Emilia,
    I'll use that tongue I have. If wit flow from't
    As boldness from my bosom, let't not be doubted
    I shall do good.

EMILIA        Now be you blest for it!
    I'll to the queen. Please you, come something nearer.

GAOLER
    Madam, if't please the queen to send the babe,
    I know not what I shall incur to pass it,
    Having no warrant.

PAULINA           You need not fear it, sir.
    This child was prisoner to the womb and is
    By law and process of great nature thence
    Freed and enfranchised, not a party to
    The anger of the king nor guilty of,
    If any be, the trespass of the queen.

GAOLER
    I do believe it.

PAULINA
    Do not you fear. Upon mine honor, I
    Will stand betwixt you and danger.         *Exeunt.*

*

44 *free* voluntary   47 *presently* at once   49 *hammered of* formulated   50 *tempt* try to win over

*Enter Leontes, Servants, Antigonus, and Lords.*　　II, iii

LEONTES

Nor night nor day no rest. It is but weakness
To bear the matter thus – mere weakness. If
The cause were not in being – part o' th' cause,
She, th' adulteress; for the harlot king　　　　　4
Is quite beyond mine arm, out of the blank　　　5
And level of my brain, plot-proof. But she
I can hook to me. Say that she were gone,
Given to the fire, a moiety of my rest　　　　　8
Might come to me again. Who's there?

SERVANT　　　　　　　　　　　　My lord.

LEONTES

How does the boy?

SERVANT　　　　　He took good rest to-night.
'Tis hoped his sickness is discharged.

LEONTES

To see his nobleness!
Conceiving the dishonor of his mother,
He straight declined, drooped, took it deeply,
Fastened and fixed the shame on't in himself,　　15
Threw off his spirit, his appetite, his sleep,
And downright languished. Leave me solely. Go　17
See how he fares.　　　　　　　*[Exit Servant.]*
　　　　　　　Fie, fie! no thought of him!　　18
The very thought of my revenges that way
Recoil upon me – in himself too mighty,
And in his parties, his alliance. Let him be
Until a time may serve. For present vengeance,
Take it on her. Camillo and Polixenes
Laugh at me, make their pastime at my sorrow.
They should not laugh if I could reach them, nor
Shall she within my power.

---

II, iii The palace of Leontes　4 *harlot* (originally of either sex)　5–6
*blank And level* target and aim　8 *moiety* part　15 *on't* of it　17 *solely* alone
18 *him* i.e. Polixenes

*Enter Paulina [with a Babe].*

LORD                     You must not enter.

PAULINA

27    Nay, rather, good my lords, be second to me.
Fear you his tyrannous passion more, alas,
Than the queen's life? a gracious innocent soul,
30    More free than he is jealous.

ANTIGONUS            That's enough.

SERVANT

Madam, he hath not slept to-night, commanded
None should come at him.

PAULINA          Not so hot, good sir.
I come to bring him sleep. 'Tis such as you,
That creep like shadows by him and do sigh
At each his needless heavings, such as you
Nourish the cause of his awaking. I
Do come with words as medicinal as true,
38    Honest as either, to purge him of that humor
That presses him from sleep.

LEONTES         What noise there, ho?

PAULINA

No noise, my lord, but needful conference
41    About some gossips for your highness.

LEONTES           How?
Away with that audacious lady! Antigonus,
I charged thee that she should not come about me.
I knew she would.

ANTIGONUS    I told her so, my lord,
On your displeasure's peril and on mine,
She should not visit you.

LEONTES        What, canst not rule her?

PAULINA

From all dishonesty he can. In this,
Unless he take the course that you have done,

---

**27** *be second to* assist   **30** *free* innocent   **38** *that humor* that of the four humors which, by having become predominant, prevented sleep   **41** *gossips* godparents for the child

Commit me for committing honor, trust it, 49
He shall not rule me.

ANTIGONUS          La you now, you hear!
When she will take the rein I let her run,
But she'll not stumble.

PAULINA                    Good my liege, I come –
And I beseech you hear me, who professes
Myself your loyal servant, your physician,
Your most obedient counsellor, yet that dares
Less appear so in comforting your evils 56
Than such as most seem yours – I say I come
From your good queen.

LEONTES                    Good queen?

PAULINA                              Good queen, my lord,
Good queen. I say good queen,
And would by combat make her good, so were I
A man, the worst about you.

LEONTES    ·               Force her hence.

PAULINA
Let him that makes but trifles of his eyes
First hand me. On mine own accord I'll off,
But first I'll do my errand. The good queen,
For she is good, hath brought you forth a daughter –
Here 'tis – commends it to your blessing.
        *[Lays down the child.]*

LEONTES                              Out!
A mankind witch! Hence with her, out o' door! 67
A most intelligencing bawd. 68

PAULINA                    Not so.
I am as ignorant in that as you
In so entitling me – and no less honest
Than you are mad, which is enough, I'll warrant,
As this world goes, to pass for honest.

LEONTES                    Traitors!
Will you not push her out? Give her the bastard.

49 *Commit* imprison   56 *comforting* condoning   67 *mankind* masculine
68 *intelligencing* spying

74   Thou dotard, thou art woman-tired, unroosted
75   By thy dame Partlet here. Take up the bastard.
      Take't up, I say. Give't to thy crone.

PAULINA                For ever
      Unvenerable be thy hands, if thou
78   Tak'st up the princess by that forcèd baseness
      Which he has put upon't!

LEONTES            He dreads his wife.

PAULINA
      So I would you did. Then 'twere past all doubt
      You'ld call your children yours.

LEONTES           A nest of traitors!

ANTIGONUS
      I am none, by this good light.

PAULINA           Nor I, nor any
      But one that's here, and that's himself; for he
      The sacred honor of himself, his queen's,
      His hopeful son's, his babe's, betrays to slander,
      Whose sting is sharper than the sword's; and will not –
      For, as the case now stands, it is a curse
      He cannot be compelled to't – once remove
      The root of his opinion, which is rotten
      As ever oak or stone was sound.

90 LEONTES         A callet
      Of boundless tongue, who late hath beat her husband
      And now baits me! This brat is none of mine;
      It is the issue of Polixenes.
      Hence with it, and together with the dam
      Commit them to the fire!

PAULINA           It is yours,
      And, might we lay th' old proverb to your charge,
      So like you 'tis the worse. Behold, my lords.
      Although the print be little, the whole matter

---

74 *dotard* imbecile; *woman-tired, unroosted* henpecked, driven from the roost  75 *Partlet* Pertelote (the hen in Chaucer's Nun's Priest's Tale, whose dominance of her husband almost brought his ruin)  78 *forcèd baseness* false designation as bastard  90 *callet* scold

And copy of the father – eye, nose, lip,
The trick of's frown, his forehead, nay, the valley,       100
The pretty dimples of his chin and cheek, his smiles,
The very mould and frame of hand, nail, finger.
And thou, good goddess Nature, which hast made it
So like to him that got it, if thou hast                   104
The ordering of the mind too, 'mongst all colors
No yellow in't, lest she suspect, as he does,              106
Her children not her husband's!                            107

LEONTES                      A gross hag!
And, lozel, thou art worthy to be hanged                   108
That wilt not stay her tongue.

ANTIGONUS                    Hang all the husbands
That cannot do that feat, you'll leave yourself
Hardly one subject.

LEONTES              Once more, take her hence!

PAULINA
A most unworthy and unnatural lord
Can do no more.

LEONTES          I'll ha' thee burnt.

PAULINA                     I care not.
It is an heretic that makes the fire,
Not she which burns in't. I'll not call you tyrant;        115
But this most cruel usage of your queen,
Not able to produce more accusation
Than your own weak-hinged fancy, something savors
Of tyranny and will ignoble make you,
Yea, scandalous to the world.

LEONTES                     On your allegiance,
Out of the chamber with her! Were I a tyrant,
Where were her life? She durst not call me so
If she did know me one. Away with her!

---

100 *valley* cleft in chin (?), crease in forehead (?)   104 *got* begot   106
*yellow* (the color of jealousy)   107 (in her righteous rage Paulina fails
to realize that jealousy would not in a wife engender doubts as to the
father of her children)   108 *lozel* worthless person   115 *tyrant* (the worst
term of abuse applied to a monarch)

PAULINA

I pray you do not push me; I'll be gone.
Look to your babe, my lord; 'tis yours. Jove send her
126  A better guiding spirit. What needs these hands?
You that are thus so tender o'er his follies
Will never do him good, not one of you.
So, so. Farewell; we are gone.                    *Exit.*

LEONTES

130  Thou, traitor, hast set on thy wife to this.
My child? away with't! Even thou, that hast
A heart so tender o'er it, take it hence
And see it instantly consumed with fire –
Even thou and none but thou. Take it up straight.
Within this hour bring me word 'tis done,
And by good testimony, or I'll seize thy life,
With what thou else call'st thine. If thou refuse
And wilt encounter with my wrath, say so.
139  The bastard brains with these my proper hands
Shall I dash out. Go, take it to the fire,
For thou set'st on thy wife.

ANTIGONUS                    I did not, sir.
These lords, my noble fellows, if they please,
Can clear me in't.

LORDS                  We can. My royal liege,
He is not guilty of her coming hither.

LEONTES

You're liars all.

LORD

Beseech your highness, give us better credit.
147  We have always truly served you, and beseech'
So to esteem of us; and on our knees we beg,
As recompense of our dear services
Past and to come, that you do change this purpose,
Which being so horrible, so bloody, must
Lead on to some foul issue. We all kneel.

126 *these hands* i.e. those which push her   130 *Thou* i.e. Antigonus   139
*proper* own   147 *beseech'* (with 'you' understood)

LEONTES

I am a feather for each wind that blows.
Shall I live on to see this bastard kneel
And call me father? Better burn it now
Than curse it then. But be it; let it live. 156
It shall not neither. You, sir, come you hither,
You that have been so tenderly officious
With Lady Margery, your midwife there, 159
To save this bastard's life – for 'tis a bastard,
So sure as this beard's grey. What will you adventure
To save this brat's life?

ANTIGONUS Anything, my lord,
That my ability may undergo 163
And nobleness impose. At least thus much.
I'll pawn the little blood which I have left 165
To save the innocent. Anything possible.

LEONTES

It shall be possible. Swear by this sword
Thou wilt perform my bidding.

ANTIGONUS I will, my lord.

LEONTES

Mark and perform it, seest thou; for the fail 169
Of any point in't shall not only be
Death to thyself but to thy lewd-tongued wife,
Whom for this time we pardon. We enjoin thee,
As thou art liege-man to us, that thou carry
This female bastard hence, and that thou bear it
To some remote and desert place quite out
Of our dominions, and that there thou leave it,
Without more mercy, to it own protection 177
And favor of the climate. As by strange fortune 178
It came to us, I do in justice charge thee,

---

**156** *be it* so be it   **159** *Margery* hen (?) (Patridge records a cant term from
ca. 1570, 'Margery-prater' hen; cf. *Partlet*, l. 75)   **163** *undergo* perform
**165** *pawn* risk   **169** *fail* failure   **177** *it* its (an earlier form of the possessive)
**178** *strange* foreign (Polixenes, whom he declares the father, a foreigner)

On thy soul's peril and thy body's torture,
181  That thou commend it strangely to some place
Where chance may nurse or end it. Take it up.

ANTIGONUS
I swear to do this, though a present death
Had been more merciful. Come on, poor babe.
Some powerful spirit instruct the kites and ravens
To be thy nurses. Wolves and bears, they say,
Casting their savageness aside, have done
Like offices of pity. Sir, be prosperous
189  In more than this deed does require. And blessing
Against this cruelty fight on thy side,
Poor thing, condemned to loss.          *Exit [with the Babe].*

LEONTES                          No, I'll not rear
Another's issue.
                    *Enter a Servant.*

SERVANT          Please your highness, posts
From those you sent to th' oracle are come
An hour since. Cleomenes and Dion,
Being well arrived from Delphos, are both landed,
Hasting to th' court.

LORD                  So please you, sir, their speed
197  Hath been beyond account.

LEONTES                          Twenty-three days
They have been absent. 'Tis good speed, foretells
199  The great Apollo suddenly will have
The truth of this appear. Prepare you, lords;
Summon a session, that we may arraign
Our most disloyal lady, for, as she hath
Been publicly accused, so shall she have
A just and open trial. While she lives
My heart will be a burthen to me. Leave me,
And think upon my bidding.                    *Exeunt.*

*

181 *commend . . . place* commit it to some foreign place  189 *require* deserve
197 *account* record    199 *suddenly* at once

*Enter Cleomenes and Dion.*                                    III, i

CLEOMENES

    The climate's delicate, the air most sweet,
    Fertile the isle, the temple much surpassing          2
    The common praise it bears.

DION                                    I shall report,
    For most it caught me, the celestial habits –
    Methinks I so should term them – and the reverence
    Of the grave wearers. O, the sacrifice,
    How ceremonious, solemn, and unearthly
    It was i' th' off'ring!

CLEOMENES               But of all, the burst
    And the ear-deaf'ning voice o' th' oracle,
    Kin to Jove's thunder, so surprised my sense
    That I was nothing.

DION                          If th' event o' th' journey
    Prove as successful to the queen – O be't so! –
    As it hath been to us rare, pleasant, speedy,
    The time is worth the use on't.                       14

CLEOMENES                          Great Apollo
    Turn all to th' best! These proclamations,
    So forcing faults upon Hermione,
    I little like.

DION            The violent carriage of it
    Will clear or end the business. When the oracle,
    Thus by Apollo's great divine sealed up,
    Shall the contents discover, something rare
    Even then will rush to knowledge. Go. Fresh horses!
    And gracious be the issue!                    *Exeunt.*

\*

III, i A posting inn en route to Leontes' palace   2 *isle* (in making Delphi
an island, as in providing Bohemia with a seacoast, Shakespeare is following
Greene)   14 *worth . . . on't* well spent

III, ii          *Enter Leontes, Lords, Officers.*

LEONTES

This sessions, to our great grief we pronounce,
Even pushes 'gainst our heart – the party tried
The daughter of a king, our wife, and one
4    Of us too much beloved. Let us be cleared
Of being tyrannous, since we so openly
Proceed in justice, which shall have due course,
7    Even to the guilt or the purgation.
Produce the prisoner.

OFFICER

It is his highness' pleasure that the queen
Appear in person here in court. Silence!
        *[Enter] Hermione, as to her trial, [Paulina, and]*
        *Ladies.*

LEONTES

Read the indictment.

OFFICER *[reads]* Hermione, queen to the worthy Leontes, king of Sicilia, thou art here accused and arraigned
of high treason, in committing adultery with Polixenes,
king of Bohemia, and conspiring with Camillo to take
away the life of our sovereign lord the king, thy royal
17    husband; the pretense whereof being by circumstances
partly laid open, thou, Hermione, contrary to the faith
and allegiance of a true subject, didst counsel and aid
them, for their better safety, to fly away by night.

HERMIONE

Since what I am to say must be but that
Which contradicts my accusation, and
The testimony on my part no other
24    But what comes from myself, it shall scarce boot me
To say, 'Not guilty.' Mine integrity,
Being counted falsehood, shall, as I express it,
Be so received. But thus: if powers divine

III, ii A public tribunal in Sicilia   4 *Of* by   7 *purgation* clearing   17
*pretense* purpose   24 *boot* profit

Behold our human actions, as they do,
I doubt not then but innocence shall make
False accusation blush and tyranny
Tremble at patience. You, my lord, best know,
Who least will seem to do so, my past life
Hath been as continent, as chaste, as true,
As I am now unhappy; which is more
Than history can pattern, though devised                    35
And played to take spectators. For behold me –             36
A fellow of the royal bed, which owe                        37
A moiety of the throne, a great king's daughter,           38
The mother to a hopeful prince – here standing
To prate and talk for life and honor 'fore
Who please to come and hear. For life, I prize it
As I weigh grief, which I would spare. For honor,
'Tis a derivative from me to mine,                          43
And only that I stand for. I appeal
To your own conscience, sir, before Polixenes
Came to your court, how I was in your grace,
How merited to be so; since he came,
With what encounter so uncurrent I                          48
Have strained t' appear thus; if one jot beyond            49
The bound of honor, or in act or will
That way inclining, hardened be the hearts
Of all that hear me, and my near'st of kin
Cry fie upon my grave!

LEONTES                    I ne'er heard yet
  That any of these bolder vices wanted
  Less impudence to gainsay what they did
  Than to perform it first.

HERMIONE                    That's true enough,
  Though 'tis a saying, sir, not due to me.                 57

---

35 *pattern* match  36 *take* please  37 *owe* own  38 *moiety* share  43 *a
derivative . . . mine* something to be inherited by my children from me  48
*uncurrent* unlawful  49 *strained* sinned  57 *due to me* applicable to my
behavior

LEONTES
    You will not own it.

58 HERMIONE          More than mistress of
    Which comes to me in name of fault, I must not
    At all acknowledge. For Polixenes,
    With whom I am accused, I do confess
62     I loved him as in honor he required –
    With such a kind of love as might become
    A lady like me, with a love even such,
    So and no other, as yourself commanded –
    Which not to have done I think had been in me
    Both disobedience and ingratitude
    To you and toward your friend, whose love had spoke,
    Even since it could speak, from an infant, freely
    That it was yours. Now, for conspiracy,
    I know not how it tastes, though it be dished
    For me to try how. All I know of it
    Is that Camillo was an honest man;
    And why he left your court, the gods themselves,
75     Wotting no more than I, are ignorant.

LEONTES
    You knew of his departure, as you know
    What you have underta'en to do in's absence.

HERMIONE
    Sir,
    You speak a language that I understand not,
80     My life stands in the level of your dreams,
    Which I'll lay down.

LEONTES          Your actions are my dreams.
    You had a bastard by Polixenes,
    And I but dreamed it. As you were past all shame –
84     Those of your fact are so – so past all truth,
85     Which to deny concerns more than avails; for as
    Thy brat hath been cast out, like to itself,

---

58–59 *More . . . fault* more faults than I have  **62** *required* deserved  **75**
*Wotting* if they know  **80** *in* on  **84** *fact* deed  **85** *concerns* implicates

No father owning it – which is, indeed,
More criminal in thee than it – so thou
Shalt feel our justice, in whose easiest passage
Look for no less than death.

HERMIONE                    Sir, spare your threats.
The bug which you would fright me with I seek.          91
To me can life be no commodity.                         92
The crown and comfort of my life, your favor,
I do give lost, for I do feel it gone,
But know not how it went. My second joy
And first-fruits of my body, from his presence
I am barred, like one infectious. My third comfort,
Starred most unluckily, is from my breast,             98
The innocent milk in it most innocent mouth,
Haled out to murder. Myself on every post
Proclaimed a strumpet : with immodest hatred          101
The child-bed privilege denied, which 'longs
To women of all fashion. Lastly, hurried
Here to this place, i' th' open air, before
I have got strength of limit. Now, my liege,           105
Tell me what blessings I have here alive,
That I should fear to die ? Therefore proceed.
But yet hear this – mistake me not, no life            108
(I prize it not a straw) but for mine honor,
Which I would free. If I shall be condemned
Upon surmises, all proofs sleeping else
But what your jealousies awake, I tell you
'Tis rigor and not law. Your honors all,
I do refer me to the oracle.
Apollo be my judge !
LORD                    This your request
Is altogether just. Therefore bring forth,
And in Apollo's name, his oracle.
                              [*Exeunt certain Officers.*]

91 *bug* bugbear   92 *commodity* comfort   98 *Starred* fated   101 *immodest* immoderate   105 *of limit* limited   108–09 *no life . . . honor* I speak not to ask life but for my honor

67

HERMIONE
    The emperor of Russia was my father.
    O that he were alive, and here beholding
    His daughter's trial; that he did but see
121    The flatness of my misery – yet with eyes
    Of pity, not revenge.
        *[Enter Officers with] Cleomenes, [and] Dion.*

OFFICER
    You here shall swear upon this sword of justice,
    That you, Cleomenes and Dion, have
    Been both at Delphos, and from thence have brought
    This sealed-up oracle, by the hand delivered
    Of great Apollo's priest, and that since then
    You have not dared to break the holy seal
    Nor read the secrets in't.

CLEOMENES, DION      All this we swear.

LEONTES
130    Break up the seals and read.

OFFICER *[reads]* Hermione is chaste, Polixenes blame-
less, Camillo a true subject, Leontes a jealous tyrant, his
innocent babe truly begotten; and the king shall live
without an heir if that which is lost be not found.

LORDS
    Now blessèd be the great Apollo!

HERMIONE             Praisèd!

LEONTES
    Hast thou read truth?

OFFICER          Ay, my lord, even so
    As it is here set down.

LEONTES
    There is no truth at all i' th' oracle.
139    The sessions shall proceed. This is mere falsehood.
        *[Enter Servant.]*

SERVANT
    My lord the king, the king!

**121** *flatness* uniformity   **130** *up* open   **139** *sessions* trial

LEONTES                        What is the business?

SERVANT

O sir, I shall be hated to report it.
The prince your son, with mere conceit and fear          142
Of the queen's speed, is gone.          143

LEONTES                        How? gone?

SERVANT                                        Is dead.

LEONTES

Apollo's angry, and the heavens themselves
Do strike at my injustice.
          *[Hermione swoons.]*  How now there?

PAULINA

This news is mortal to the queen. Look down          146
And see what death is doing.

LEONTES                        Take her hence.

Her heart is but o'ercharged; she will recover.          148
I have too much believed mine own suspicion.
Beseech you, tenderly apply to her
Some remedies for life.
          *[Exeunt Paulina and Ladies with Hermione.]*
                        Apollo, pardon
My great profaneness 'gainst thine oracle!
I'll reconcile me to Polixenes,
New woo my queen, recall the good Camillo,
Whom I proclaim a man of truth, of mercy;
For, being transported by my jealousies
To bloody thoughts and to revenge, I chose
Camillo for the minister to poison
My friend Polixenes, which had been done,
But that the good mind of Camillo tardied
My swift command, though I with death and with
Reward did threaten and encourage him,
Not doing it and being done. He, most humane
And filled with honor, to my kingly guest

---

142 *conceit* imagination; *fear* anxiety   143 *speed* success   146 *mortal* fatal
148 *o'ercharged* too full (of grief)

165 Unclasped my practice, quit his fortunes here,
    Which you knew great, and to the hazard
167 Of all incertainties himself commended,
168 No richer than his honor. How he glisters
169 Through my rust! and how his piety
    Does my deeds make the blacker!
            [*Enter Paulina.*]
170 PAULINA                        Woe the while!
    O, cut my lace, lest my heart, cracking it,
    Break too!
    LORD          What fit is this, good lady?
    PAULINA
    What studied torments, tyrant, hast for me?
    What wheels? racks? fires? what flaying? boiling
    In leads or oils? what old or newer torture
    Must I receive, whose every word deserves
    To taste of thy most worst? Thy tyranny,
    Together working with thy jealousies,
    Fancies too weak for boys, too green and idle
    For girls of nine, O, think what they have done,
    And then run mad indeed, stark mad, for all
182 Thy bygone fooleries were but spices of it.
    That thou betrayedst Polixenes, 'twas nothing;
184 That did but show thee, of a fool, inconstant
    And damnable ingrateful. Nor was't much
    Thou wouldst have poisoned good Camillo's honor,
187 To have him kill a king—poor trespasses,
    More monstrous standing by. Whereof I reckon
    The casting forth to crows thy baby daughter
    To be or none or little, though a devil
    Would have shed water out of fire ere done't.
    Nor is't directly laid to thee, the death

---

165 *Unclasped my practice* revealed my evil design  167 *commended* entrusted  168 *glisters* shines  169 *Through* (pronounced as disyllable)  170 *while* time  182 *spices* small things  184 *of a fool* for a fool  187–88 *poor . . . by* slight sins compared to others you are guilty of

Of the young prince, whose honorable thoughts,
Thoughts high for one so tender, cleft the heart          194
That could conceive a gross and foolish sire
Blemished his gracious dam. This is not, no,
Laid to thy answer. But the last – O lords,
When I have said, cry 'Woe !' – the queen, the queen,
The sweet'st dear'st creature's dead, and vengeance for't
Not dropped down yet.

LORD                              The higher powers forbid !

PAULINA
I say she's dead ; I'll swear't. If word nor oath
Prevail not, go and see. If you can bring
Tincture or lustre in her lip, her eye,          203
Heat outwardly or breath within, I'll serve you
As I would do the gods. But, O thou tyrant,
Do not repent these things, for they are heavier
Than all thy woes can stir. Therefore betake thee          207
To nothing but despair. A thousand knees
Ten thousand years together, naked, fasting,
Upon a barren mountain, and still winter
In storm perpetual, could not move the gods
To look that way thou wert.          212

LEONTES                    Go on, go on.
Thou canst not speak too much. I have deserved
All tongues to talk their bitt'rest.

LORD                              Say no more.
Howe'er the business goes, you have made fault
I' th' boldness of your speech.

PAULINA                         I am sorry for't.
All faults I make, when I shall come to know them,
I do repent. Alas, I have showed too much
The rashness of a woman. He is touched
To the noble heart. What's gone and what's past help
Should be past grief. Do not receive affliction

---

194 *tender* i.e. young   203 *Tincture . . . eye* color to the lip or brightness to
the eye   207 *stir* alter   212 *look . . . wert* take notice of you

At my petition. I beseech you, rather
223 Let me be punished, that have minded you
Of what you should forget. Now, good my liege,
Sir, royal sir, forgive a foolish woman.
The love I bore your queen – lo, fool again ! –
I'll speak of her no more, nor of your children ;
I'll not remember you of my own lord,
229 Who is lost too. Take your patience to you,
And I'll say nothing.

LEONTES                    Thou didst speak but well
When most the truth, which I receive much better
Than to be pitied of thee. Prithee, bring me
To the dead bodies of my queen and son.
One grave shall be for both. Upon them shall
The causes of their death appear, unto
Our shame perpetual. Once a day I'll visit
The chapel where they lie, and tears shed there
238 Shall be my recreation. So long as nature
Will bear up with this exercise, so long
I daily vow to use it. Come, and lead me
To these sorrows.                    *Exeunt.*

*

III, iii                    *Enter Antigonus, [and] a Mariner, [with a] Babe.*
ANTIGONUS
1 Thou art perfect then our ship hath touched upon
The deserts of Bohemia ?
MARINER                    Ay, my lord, and fear
We have landed in ill time. The skies look grimly
4 And threaten present blusters. In my conscience,
The heavens with that we have in hand are angry
And frown upon's.

223 *minded* reminded  229 *Take . . . you* be patient  238 *recreation*
refreshing of mind and spirit
III, iii The seacoast of Bohemia  1 *perfect* sure  4 *conscience* opinion

72

ANTIGONUS
    Their sacred wills be done ! Go, get aboard ;
    Look to thy bark. I'll not be long before
    I call upon thee.
MARINER        Make your best haste, and go not
    Too far i' th' land. 'Tis like to be loud weather.
    Besides, this place is famous for the creatures
    Of prey that keep upon't.                              12
ANTIGONUS                  Go thou away ;
    I'll follow instantly.
MARINER            I am glad at heart
    To be so rid o' th' business.              *Exit.*
ANTIGONUS                   Come, poor babe.
    I have heard, but not believed, the spirits o' th' dead
    May walk again. If such thing be, thy mother
    Appeared to me last night, for ne'er was dream
    So like a waking. To me comes a creature,
    Sometimes her head on one side, some another.
    I never saw a vessel of like sorrow,
    So filled and so becoming. In pure white robes,
    Like very sanctity, she did approach
    My cabin where I lay ; thrice bowed before me,
    And, gasping to begin some speech, her eyes
    Became two spouts. The fury spent, anon           25
    Did this break her from : 'Good Antigonus,
    Since fate, against thy better disposition,
    Hath made thy person for the thrower-out
    Of my poor babe, according to thine oath,
    Places remote enough are in Bohemia ;
    There weep and leave it crying. And, for the babe
    Is counted lost for ever, Perdita,                32
    I prithee, call't. For this ungentle business,
    Put on thee by my lord, thou ne'er shalt see
    Thy wife Paulina more.' And so, with shrieks,
    She melted into air. Affrighted much,

12 *keep* live   25 *anon* presently   32 *Perdita* i.e. the lost one (feminine)

I did in time collect myself, and thought
38   This was so and no slumber. Dreams are toys;
Yet for this once, yea, superstitiously,
40   I will be squared by this. I do believe
Hermione hath suffered death, and that
Apollo would, this being indeed the issue
Of King Polixenes, it should here be laid,
Either for life or death, upon the earth
Of its right father. Blossom, speed thee well.
46   There lie, and there thy character; there these,
47   Which may, if fortune please, both breed thee, pretty,
And still rest thine. The storm begins. Poor wretch,
That for thy mother's fault art thus exposed
To loss and what may follow. Weep I cannot,
But my heart bleeds; and most accursed am I
To be by oath enjoined to this. Farewell!
The day frowns more and more. Thou'rt like to have
A lullaby too rough. I never saw
The heavens so dim by day. A savage clamor!
Well may I get aboard! This is the chase.
I am gone for ever.        *Exit, pursued by a bear.*
     *[Enter] Shepherd.*

58 SHEPHERD   I would there were no age between ten and
three-and-twenty, or that youth would sleep out the rest;
for there is nothing in the between but getting wenches
61   with child, wronging the ancientry, stealing, fighting.
Hark you now. Would any but these boiled brains of
nineteen and two-and-twenty hunt this weather? They
have scared away two of my best sheep, which I fear the
wolf will sooner find than the master. If anywhere I have
them, 'tis by the seaside, browsing of ivy. Good luck,
an't be thy will! What have we here? Mercy on's, a

---

**38** *toys* trifles   **40** *squared* ruled   **46** *character* writing; *these* i.e. gold and
the jewels by which she is later to be identified   **47** *breed* rear   **58** (As *ten*
seems too tender an age to indulge in some of the escapades referred to,
some editors change 'ten' to 'sixteen'. If written in Arabic numerals,
either 16 or 19 might easily be misread 10. Cf. l. 63.)   **61** *ancientry* old
people

barne, a very pretty barne! A boy or a child, I wonder? 68
A pretty one, a very pretty one. Sure, some scape. 69
Though I am not bookish, yet I can read waiting-gentle-
woman in the scape. This has been some stair-work,
some trunk-work, some behind-door-work. They were 72
warmer that got this than the poor thing is here. I'll take 73
it up for pity. Yet I'll tarry till my son come. He hal-
looed but even now. Whoa, ho, hoa!                    75
　　　*Enter Clown.*

CLOWN Hilloa, loa!

SHEPHERD What, art so near? If thou'lt see a thing to
talk on when thou art dead and rotten, come hither.
What ail'st thou, man?

CLOWN I have seen two such sights, by sea and by land –
but I am not to say it is a sea, for it is now the sky; betwixt the firmament and it you cannot thrust a bodkin's
point.

SHEPHERD Why, boy, how is it?

CLOWN I would you did but see how it chafes, how it
rages, how it takes up the shore. But that's not to the
point. O, the most piteous cry of the poor souls! Sometimes to see 'em, and not to see 'em. Now the ship
boring the moon with her main-mast, and anon swallowed with yest and froth, as you'ld thrust a cork into a 89
hogshead. And then for the land-service – to see how 90
the bear tore out his shoulder-bone, how he cried to me
for help and said his name was Antigonus, a nobleman.
But to make an end of the ship – to see how the sea flap- 93
dragoned it. But, first, how the poor souls roared, and
the sea mocked them, and how the poor gentleman
roared and the bear mocked him, both roaring louder
than the sea or weather.

---

**68** *child* girl　**69** *scape* escapade　**72** *trunk-work* a pun on 'trunk' meaning
(1) a secret place, (2) the body apart from head and limbs　**73** *got* begot
**75** s.d. *Clown* country fellow　**89** *yest* foam　**90** *land-service* (1) a dish of
food served on land, (2) the branch of the military serving on land, not at
sea　**93** *flap-dragoned* swallowed whole

SHEPHERD Name of mercy, when was this, boy?

CLOWN Now, now; I have not winked since I saw these
100    sights. The men are not yet cold under water, nor the
    bear half dined on the gentleman. He's at it now.

SHEPHERD Would I had been by, to have helped the old
    man.

CLOWN I would you had been by the ship side, to have
    helped her. There your charity would have lacked
    footing.

SHEPHERD Heavy matters, heavy matters! But look thee
    here, boy. Now bless thyself! thou mettest with things
    dying, I with things new-born. Here's a sight for thee.
108    Look thee, a bearing-cloth for a squire's child. Look
    thee here. Take up, take up, boy; open't. So, let's see. It
    was told me I should be rich by the fairies. This is some
111    changeling. Open't. What's within, boy?

CLOWN You're a made old man. If the sins of your youth
113    are forgiven you, you're well to live. Gold! all gold!

SHEPHERD This is fairy gold, boy, and 'twill prove so. Up
115    with't, keep it close. Home, home, the next way. We are
    lucky, boy, and to be so still requires nothing but secrecy.
    Let my sheep go. Come, good boy, the next way home.

CLOWN Go you the next way with your findings. I'll go
    see if the bear be gone from the gentleman and how
120    much he hath eaten. They are never curst but when they
    are hungry. If there be any of him left, I'll bury it.

SHEPHERD That's a good deed. If thou mayest discern by
    that which is left of him what he is, fetch me to the sight
    of him.

CLOWN Marry, will I; and you shall help to put him i' the
    ground.

SHEPHERD 'Tis a lucky day, boy, and we'll do good deeds
    on't.                                                    *Exeunt.*

*

100 *cold* dead    108 *bearing-cloth* cloth or mantle in which a child is carried
to baptism    111 *changeling* child taken or left by fairies    113 *well to live*
well-to-do    115 *close* secret; *next* nearest    120 *curst* mean

*Enter Time, the Chorus.*

TIME

I, that please some, try all, both joy and terror          1
Of good and bad, that makes and unfolds error,          2
Now take upon me, in the name of Time,
To use my wings. Impute it not a crime
To me or my swift passage that I slide
O'er sixteen years and leave the growth untried          6
Of that wide gap, since it is in my power
To o'erthrow law and in one self-born hour
To plant and o'erwhelm custom. Let me pass
The same I am, ere ancient'st order was
Or what is now received. I witness to
The times that brought them in. So shall I do
To the freshest things now reigning, and make stale
The glistering of this present, as my tale          14
Now seems to it. Your patience this allowing,
I turn my glass and give my scene such growing
As you had slept between. Leontes leaving,
Th' effects of his fond jealousies so grieving          18
That he shuts up himself, imagine me,
Gentle spectators, that I now may be
In fair Bohemia. And remember well,
I mentioned a son o' th' king's, which Florizel
I now name to you, and with speed so pace          23
To speak of Perdita, now grown in grace
Equal with wond'ring. What of her ensues
I list not prophesy; but let Time's news          26
Be known when 'tis brought forth. A shepherd's daughter

IV, i (Because of its awkwardness in both verse and thought, some editors
have accepted Heath's view that this chorus is an interpolation written by
one other than Shakespeare. Professor Kittredge defends its authenticity,
declaring it written to fit the character of 'Father Time – a doddering,
toothless ancient, halting but fluent, senile but self-assured, ridiculous
but triumphant.') 1 *try* test  1–2 *joy . . . bad* joy to good men and terror
to bad  2 *unfolds* reveals  6 *growth untried* events untold  14 *glistering*
brightness  18 *fond* foolish  23 *pace* proceed  26 *list not* do not wish to

28 And what to her adheres, which follows after,

29 Is th' argument of Time. Of this allow
If ever you have spent time worse ere now;
If never, yet that Time himself doth say
He wishes earnestly you never may.      *Exit.*

IV, ii      *Enter Polixenes and Camillo.*

POLIXENES   I pray thee, good Camillo, be no more importunate. 'Tis a sickness denying thee anything, a death to grant this.

CAMILLO   It is fifteen years since I saw my country.
5    Though I have for the most part been aired abroad, I desire to lay my bones there. Besides, the penitent king, my master, hath sent for me, to whose feeling sorrows I
8    might be some allay – or I o'erween to think so – which is another spur to my departure.

POLIXENES   As thou lov'st me, Camillo, wipe not out the rest of thy services by leaving me now. The need I have of thee thine own goodness hath made. Better not to
13   have had thee than thus to want thee. Thou, having made me businesses which none without thee can sufficiently manage, must either stay to execute them thyself or take away with thee the very services thou hast done, which if I have not enough considered – as too much I cannot – to be more thankful to thee shall be my
19   study, and my profit therein the heaping friendships. Of that fatal country, Sicilia, prithee speak no more, whose very naming punishes me with the remembrance of that penitent, as thou call'st him, and reconciled king, my brother, whose loss of his most precious queen and children are even now to be afresh lamented. Say to me, when saw'st thou the Prince Florizel, my son?

---

28 *adheres* relates    29 *argument* story
IV, ii The palace of the King of Bohemia    5 *been aired* lived    8 *o'erween* am
presumptuous    13 *want* be without    19 *heaping* full

Kings are no less unhappy, their issue not being gracious, than they are in losing them when they have ap-   27
proved their virtues.

CAMILLO Sir, it is three days since I saw the prince.
What his happier affairs may be, are to me unknown,
but I have missingly noted he is of late much retired   30
from court and is less frequent to his princely exercises
than formerly he hath appeared.

POLIXENES I have considered so much, Camillo, and
with some care – so far that I have eyes under my service   34
which look upon his removedness, from whom I have
this intelligence, that he is seldom from the house of a   36
most homely shepherd, a man, they say, that from very   37
nothing, and beyond the imagination of his neighbors,
is grown into an unspeakable estate.                   39

CAMILLO I have heard, sir, of such a man, who hath a
daughter of most rare note. The report of her is extended more than can be thought to begin from such a
cottage.

POLIXENES That's likewise part of my intelligence; but,
I fear, the angle that plucks our son thither. Thou shalt   44
accompany us to the place, where we will, not appearing
what we are, have some question with the shepherd, from
whose simplicity I think it not uneasy to get the cause of
my son's resort thither. Prithee be my present partner
in this business, and lay aside the thoughts of Sicilia.

CAMILLO I willingly obey your command.

POLIXENES My best Camillo! We must disguise ourselves.                                    *Exeunt*.

*

27 *approved* proved   30 *missingly* in missing him   34 *eyes* spies   36
*intelligence* report   37 *homely* unpretentious   39 *unspeakable estate* untold
wealth   44 *angle* fishhook

**IV, iii**     *Enter Autolycus, singing.*

1     When daffodils begin to peer,
2         With heigh! the doxy over the dale,
      Why, then comes in the sweet o' the year,
4         For the red blood reigns in the winter's pale.

      The white sheet bleaching on the hedge,
          With heigh! the sweet birds, O how they sing!
7     Doth set my pugging tooth on edge,
          For a quart of ale is a dish for a king.

      The lark, that tirra-lyra chants,
          With heigh! with heigh! the thrush and the jay,
11    Are summer songs for me and my aunts,
          While we lie tumbling in the hay.

13    I have served Prince Florizel and in my time wore three-
      pile, but now I am out of service.

      But shall I go mourn for that, my dear?
          The pale moon shines by night.
      And when I wander here and there,
          I then do most go right.

      If tinkers may have leave to live,
20        And bear the sow-skin budget,
      Then my account I well may give,
          And in the stocks avouch it.

23    My traffic is sheets; when the kite builds, look to lesser
      linen. My father named me Autolycus, who being, as I
25    am, littered under Mercury, was likewise a snapper-up
26    of unconsidered trifles. With die and drab I purchased

---

**IV, iii** A footpath in Bohemia   **1** *peer* appear   **2** *doxy* female beggar, pros-
titute   **4** *in the winter's pale* (1) instead of winter's pallor, (2) in winter's
domain   **7** *pugging* pilfering (?) (cf. sweet tooth)   **11** *aunts* i.e. prostitutes
**13** *three-pile* the finest velvet   **20** *budget* sack   **23** *lesser* smaller pieces of
**25** *littered under Mercury* born when the planet Mercury was in the ascendant (as Mercury was the god of thieving, both the earlier Autolycus,
father of Odysseus, and this his namesake are skilled in that art)   **26–27**
*With . . . caparison* by dice and harlots I got this attire

80

this caparison, and my revenue is the silly cheat. Gal- 27
lows and knock are too powerful on the highway;
beating and hanging are terrors to me. For the life to
come, I sleep out the thought of it. A prize! a prize! 30
    *Enter Clown.*

CLOWN Let me see; every 'leven wether tods; every tod 31
yields pound and odd shilling; fifteen hundred shorn,
what comes the wool to?

AUTOLYCUS [*aside*] If the springe hold, the cock's mine.

CLOWN I cannot do't without counters. Let me see; what
am I to buy for our sheep-shearing feast? Three pound
of sugar, five pound of currants, rice – what will this
sister of mine do with rice? But my father hath made her
mistress of the feast, and she lays it on. She hath made me
four and twenty nosegays for the shearers – three-man 40
songmen all, and very good ones; but they are most of
them means and bases, but one puritan amongst them, 42
and he sings psalms to hornpipes. I must have saffron to
color the warden pies; mace; dates? –none, that's out of 44
my note; nutmegs, seven; a race or two of ginger, but 45
that I may beg; four pounds of prunes, and as many of
raisins o' the sun. 47

AUTOLYCUS O that ever I was born!
    [*Grovels on the ground.*]

CLOWN I' the name of me –

AUTOLYCUS O, help me, help me! pluck but off these
rags, and then death, death!

CLOWN Alack, poor soul, thou hast need of more rags to
lay on thee, rather than have these off.

AUTOLYCUS O, sir, the loathsomeness of them offends
me more than the stripes I have received, which are
mighty ones and millions.

---

**27** *revenue* source of income   **30** *prize* booty or one from whom it may be
taken   **31** *'leven wether tods* eleven sheep yield a tod (an old weight for wool)
**40–41** *three-man songmen* men who sing catches or rounds   **42** *means* tenors
**44** *warden* pear   **44–45** *out . . . note* not on my list   **45** *race* root   **47** *o' the
sun* sun-dried

CLOWN Alas, poor man! A million of beating may come to a great matter.

AUTOLYCUS I am robbed, sir, and beaten, my money
60 and apparel ta'en from me, and these detestable things put upon me.

CLOWN What, by a horseman, or a footman?

AUTOLYCUS A footman, sweet sir, a footman.

CLOWN Indeed, he should be a footman by the garments he has left with thee. If this be a horseman's coat, it hath seen very hot service. Lend my thy hand, I'll help thee. Come, lend me thy hand.

    *[Helps him up.]*

AUTOLYCUS O, good sir, tenderly. O!

CLOWN Alas, poor soul!

70 AUTOLYCUS O, good sir, softly, good sir. I fear, sir, my shoulder-blade is out.

CLOWN How now? canst stand?

AUTOLYCUS *[picking his pocket]* Softly, dear sir; good sir, softly. You ha' done me a charitable office.

CLOWN Dost lack any money? I have a little money for thee.

AUTOLYCUS No, good sweet sir; no, I beseech you, sir. I have a kinsman not past three quarters of a mile hence, unto whom I was going. I shall there have money, or anything I want. Offer me no money, I pray you; that kills my heart.

CLOWN What manner of fellow was he that robbed you?

AUTOLYCUS A fellow, sir, that I have known to go about
83 with troll-my-dames. I knew him once a servant of the prince. I cannot tell, good sir, for which of his virtues it was, but he was certainly whipped out of the court.

CLOWN His vices, you would say. There's no virtue whipped out of the court. They cherish it to make it stay there, and yet it will no more but abide.

AUTOLYCUS Vices, I would say, sir. I know this man

83 *troll-my-dames* a game resembling bagatelle

well. He hath been since an ape-bearer, then a process-
server, a bailiff. Then he compassed a motion of the 91
Prodigal Son, and married a tinker's wife within a mile
where my land and living lies, and, having flown over
many knavish professions, he settled only in rogue.
Some call him Autolycus.

CLOWN Out upon him! Prig, for my life, prig! He haunts 96
wakes, fairs, and bear-baitings.

AUTOLYCUS Very true, sir; he, sir, he. That's the rogue
that put me into this apparel.

CLOWN Not a more cowardly rogue in all Bohemia. If you
had but looked big and spit at him, he'ld have run.

AUTOLYCUS I must confess to you, sir, I am no fighter. I
am false of heart that way, and that he knew, I warrant
him.

CLOWN How do you now?

AUTOLYCUS Sweet sir, much better than I was. I can
stand and walk. I will even take my leave of you and
pace softly towards my kinsman's.

CLOWN Shall I bring thee on the way?

AUTOLYCUS No, good-faced sir; no, sweet sir.

CLOWN Then fare thee well. I must go buy spices for our
sheep-shearing.

AUTOLYCUS Prosper you, sweet sir.          *Exit [Clown].*
Your purse is not hot enough to purchase your spice.
I'll be with you at your sheep-shearing too. If I make
not this cheat bring out another and the shearers prove 115
sheep, let me be unrolled and my name put in the book 116
of virtue.
                    *Song.*

> Jog on, jog on, the foot-path way,
>     And merrily hent the stile-a.
> A merry heart goes all the day,                    119
>     Your sad tires in a mile-a.                    *Exit.*

*

91 *compassed a motion* devised a puppet-show   96 *Prig* thief   115 *bring out*
lead to   116 *unrolled* removed from the roll of thieves   119 *hent* take hold of

**IV, iv**          *Enter Florizel, Perdita.*

FLORIZEL
These your unusual weeds to each part of you

2    Do give a life – no shepherdess, but Flora

3    Peering in April's front. This your sheep-shearing
Is as a meeting of the petty gods,
And you the queen on't.

PERDITA                    Sir, my gracious lord,

6    To chide at your extremes it not becomes me –
O, pardon, that I name them. Your high self,

8    The gracious mark o' th' land, you have obscured

9    With a swain's wearing, and me, poor lowly maid,

10   Most goddess-like pranked up. But that our feasts
In every mess have folly, and the feeders
Digest it with a custom, I should blush
To see you so attired, swoon, I think,
To show myself a glass.

FLORIZEL                    I bless the time
When my good falcon made her flight across
Thy father's ground.

PERDITA                    Now Jove afford you cause!
To me the difference forges dread; your greatness
Hath not been used to fear. Even now I tremble
To think your father, by some accident,
Should pass this way as you did. O, the Fates!
How would he look, to see his work, so noble,
Vilely bound up? What would he say? Or how
Should I, in these my borrowed flaunts, behold
The sternness of his presence?

FLORIZEL                    Apprehend
Nothing but jollity. The gods themselves,
Humbling their deities to love, have taken

---

IV, iv The Shepherd's garden  2 *Flora* the goddess of flowers  3 *April's front* early April  6 *extremes* exaggerations  8 *mark* ornament  9 *wearing* clothes  10 *pranked up* made fine

The shapes of beasts upon them. Jupiter 27
Became a bull, and bellowed; the green Neptune
A ram, and bleated; and the fire-robed god,
Golden Apollo, a poor humble swain,
As I seem now. Their transformations
Were never for a piece of beauty rarer,
Nor in a way so chaste, since my desires
Run not before mine honor, nor my lusts 34
Burn hotter than my faith.

PERDITA O, but, sir,
Your resolution cannot hold when 'tis
Opposed, as it must be, by th' power of the king.
One of these two must be necessities,
Which then will speak, that you must change this
    purpose,
Or I my life.

FLORIZEL Thou dearest Perdita,
With these forced thoughts, I prithee, darken not 41
The mirth o' th' feast. Or I'll be thine, my fair, 42
Or not my father's. For I cannot be
Mine own, nor anything to any, if
I be not thine. To this I am most constant,
Though destiny say no. Be merry, gentle;
Strangle such thoughts as these with anything
That you behold the while. Your guests are coming.
Lift up your countenance, as it were the day
Of celebration of that nuptial which
We two have sworn shall come.

PERDITA O lady Fortune,
Stand you auspicious!

FLORIZEL See, your guests approach.

27–30 (Jupiter took the shape of a bull to carry off Europa, Neptune that of a ram to woo Theophane; and Apollo, exiled from heaven by Jupiter, served Admetus as a shepherd and enabled him to win Alcestis.) 34 *Run not before* i.e. do not win a victory over 41 *forced* far-fetched 42 *Or* either

Address yourself to entertain them sprightly,
And let's be red with mirth.
   *[Enter] Shepherd, Clown, [with] Polixenes, [and]*
    *Camillo [disguised], Mopsa, Dorcas, Servants.*

**SHEPHERD**
 Fie, daughter! When my old wife lived, upon
56 This day she was both pantler, butler, cook,
 Both dame and servant; welcomed all, served all;
 Would sing her song and dance her turn; now here
 At upper end o' th' table, now i' th' middle;
 On his shoulder, and his; her face o' fire
 With labor, and the thing she took to quench it
 She would to each one sip. You are retirèd,
63 As if you were a feasted one and not
 The hostess of the meeting. Pray you bid
 These unknown friends to 's welcome, for it is
 A way to make us better friends, more known.
 Come, quench your blushes and present yourself
 That which you are, mistress o' th' feast. Come on,
 And bid us welcome to your sheep-shearing,
 As your good flock shall prosper.

**PERDITA** *[to Polixenes]*   Sir, welcome.
 It is my father's will I should take on me
 The hostess-ship o' th' day.
   *[To Camillo]*   You're welcome, sir.
 Give me those flowers there, Dorcas. Reverend sirs,
74 For you there's rosemary and rue; these keep
 Seeming and savor all the winter long.
 Grace and remembrance be to you both,
 And welcome to our shearing!

**POLIXENES**     Shepherdess –
 A fair one are you – well you fit our ages
 With flowers of winter.

**PERDITA**    Sir, the year growing ancient,
 Not yet on summer's death nor on the birth

---

**56** *pantler* pantry-servant **63** *feasted one* i.e. guest **74** *rosemary . . . rue*
(associated respectively with remembrance and grace)

Of trembling winter, the fairest flowers o' th' season
Are our carnations and streaked gillyvors,                    82
Which some call nature's bastards. Of that kind              83
Our rustic garden's barren, and I care not
To get slips of them.

POLIXENES                    Wherefore, gentle maiden,
Do you neglect them?

PERDITA                    For I have heard it said
There is an art which in their piedness shares              87
With great creating nature.

POLIXENES                    Say there be;
Yet nature is made better by no mean                        89
But nature makes that mean. So, over that art
Which you say adds to nature, is an art
That nature makes. You see, sweet maid, we marry
A gentler scion to the wildest stock,
And make conceive a bark of baser kind
By bud of nobler race. This is an art
Which does mend nature – change it rather – but
The art itself is nature.

PERDITA                    So it is.

POLIXENES
Then make your garden rich in gillyvors,
And do not call them bastards.

PERDITA                    I'll not put
The dibble in earth to set one slip of them,                100
No more than, were I painted, I would wish
This youth should say 'twere well, and only therefore
Desire to breed by me. Here's flowers for you,
Hot lavender, mints, savory, marjoram,
The marigold, that goes to bed wi' th' sun                  105
And with him rises weeping. These are flowers

---

82 *gillyvors* gillyflowers, clove pinks   83 *nature's bastards* i.e. created by
crossbreeding   87–88 *There . . . nature* i.e. the parti-color of the flower owes
as much to the skill of the gardener as to nature   89 *mean* method   100
*dibble* tool for making holes for seed   105 *goes . . . sun* i.e. closes its petals at
nightfall

Of middle summer, and I think they are given
To men of middle age. Y'are very welcome.

CAMILLO

I should leave grazing, were I of your flock,
And only live by gazing.

PERDITA                    Out, alas!
You'ld be so lean that blasts of January
Would blow you through and through. Now, my fair'st
    friend,
I would I had some flowers o' th' spring that might
Become your time of day, and yours, and yours,
That wear upon your virgin branches yet
116   Your maidenheads growing. O Proserpina,
For the flowers now that, frighted, thou let'st fall
From Dis's wagon; daffodils,
119   That come before the swallow dares, and take
The winds of March with beauty; violets dim,
121   But sweeter than the lids of Juno's eyes
122   Or Cytherea's breath; pale primroses,
That die unmarried, ere they can behold
124   Bright Phoebus in his strength – a malady
Most incident to maids; bold oxlips and
The crown imperial; lilies of all kinds,
The flower-de-luce being one. O, these I lack
To make you garlands of, and my sweet friend,
To strew him o'er and o'er!
129 FLORIZEL                    What, like a corse?
PERDITA
No, like a bank for love to lie and play on.
Not like a corse; or if, not to be buried,
But quick and in mine arms. Come, take your flowers.
Methinks I play as I have seen them do

---

116 *Proserpina* Ceres' daughter, who, spied by Dis (Pluto, god of the under-world) while she was gathering flowers, was seized and taken by him to the underworld to become his queen   119 *take* charm   121 *Juno* wife of Jupiter and queen of heaven   122 *Cytherea* Venus   124 *Phoebus* the sun (Phoebus Apollo the sun god)   129 *corse* corpse

In Whitsun pastorals. Sure this robe of mine            134
Does change my disposition.

FLORIZEL                         What you do
Still betters what is done. When you speak, sweet,
I'ld have you do it ever. When you sing,
I'ld have you buy and sell so, so give alms,
Pray so, and for the ord'ring your affairs,
To sing them too. When you do dance, I wish you
A wave o' th' sea, that you might ever do
Nothing but that, move still, still so,
And own no other function. Each your doing,            143
So singular in each particular,
Crowns what you are doing in the present deeds,
That all your acts are queens.

PERDITA                         O Doricles,            146
Your praises are too large. But that your youth,
And the true blood which peeps fairly through't,       148
Do plainly give you out an unstained shepherd,
With wisdom I might fear, my Doricles,
You wooed me the false way.

FLORIZEL                         I think you have
As little skill to fear as I have purpose              152
To put you to't. But come; our dance, I pray.
Your hand, my Perdita. So turtles pair                 154
That never mean to part.

PERDITA                    I'll swear for 'em.

POLIXENES
This is the prettiest low-born lass that ever
Ran on the greensward. Nothing she does or seems
But smacks of something greater than herself,          158
Too noble for this place.

CAMILLO                         He tells her something

134 *Whitsun pastorals* plays (or morris dances) presented around Whitsun,
the seventh Sunday after Easter   143 *Each your doing* everything you do
146 *Doricles* (the name assumed by Florizel in his disguise)   148 *peeps
fairly* (many editors insert 'so' in the belief that it may have been absorbed
in the 's' of 'peeps')   152 *skill* reason   154 *turtles* turtledoves   158
*greater* of gentler blood

160     That makes her blood look on't. Good sooth, she is
    The queen of curds and cream.

CLOWN                             Come on, strike up!

DORCAS
    Mopsa must be your mistress. Marry, garlic,
163     To mend her kissing with!

MOPSA                       Now, in good time!

CLOWN
    Not a word, a word! We stand upon our manners.
    Come, strike up!
        *[Music.] Here a dance of Shepherds and Shepherdesses.*

POLIXENES
    Pray, good shepherd, what fair swain is this
    Which dances with your daughter?

SHEPHERD
    They call him Doricles, and boasts himself
169     To have a worthy feeding. But I have it
    Upon his own report and I believe it;
171     He looks like sooth. He says he loves my daughter.
    I think so too, for never gazed the moon
    Upon the water as he'll stand and read
    As 'twere my daughter's eyes; and, to be plain,
    I think there is not half a kiss to choose
176     Who loves another best.

POLIXENES               She dances featly.

SHEPHERD
    So she does anything, though I report it
    That should be silent. If young Doricles
    Do light upon her, she shall bring him that
    Which he not dreams of.
        *Enter Servant.*

SERVANT  O master, if you did but hear the pedlar at the
    door, you would never dance again after a tabor and

---

160 *blood look on't* blush   163 *mend . . . with* escape her unpleasant breath
169 *feeding* land on which sheep feed   171 *like sooth* honest   176 *another*
the other; *featly* nimbly

pipe – no, the bagpipe could not move you. He sings
several tunes faster than you'll tell money. He utters 184
them as he had eaten ballads and all men's ears grew to
his tunes.

CLOWN He could never come better. He shall come in. I
love a ballad but even too well if it be doleful matter
merrily set down, or a very pleasant thing indeed and
sung lamentably.

SERVANT He hath songs for man or woman, of all sizes.
No milliner can so fit his customers with gloves. He has
the prettiest love-songs for maids, so without bawdry,
which is strange, with such delicate burthens of dildos 193
and fadings, 'Jump her and thump her.' And where 194
some stretch-mouthed rascal would, as it were, mean
mischief and break a foul gap into the matter, he makes
the maid to answer, 'Whoop, do me no harm, good
man'; puts him off, slights him, with 'Whoop, do me no
harm, good man.'

POLIXENES This is a brave fellow.

CLOWN Believe me, thou talkest of an admirable con- 201
ceited fellow. Has he any unbraided wares? 202

SERVANT He hath ribbons of all the colors i' th' rainbow,
points more than all the lawyers in Bohemia can learned- 204
ly handle, though they come to him by the gross – inkles, 205
caddises, cambrics, lawns. Why, he sings 'em over as 206
they were gods or goddesses. You would think a smock
were a she-angel, he so chants to the sleeve-hand and 208
the work about the square on't. 209

CLOWN Prithee bring him in, and let him approach singing.

PERDITA Forewarn him that he use no scurrilous words
in's tunes. *[Exit Servant.]*

---

184 *tell* count   193 *dildo* (a word used as a refrain in ballads)   194 *fadings*
burdens of songs   201 *conceited* witty   202 *unbraided* unfaded   204
*points* (1) points in an argument, (2) laces to fasten doublet and hose together
205 *inkles* linen tape   206 *caddises* worsted ribbons   208 *sleeve-hand* cuff
209 *square* the front upper part of a dress

213 CLOWN You have of these pedlars that have more in them
than you'ld think, sister.

PERDITA Ay, good brother, or go about to think.

*Enter Autolycus, singing.*

Lawn as white as driven snow,
217          Cyprus black as e'er was crow,
Gloves as sweet as damask roses,
Masks for faces and for noses,
220          Bugle bracelet, necklace amber,
Perfume for a lady's chamber,
222          Golden quoifs and stomachers
For my lads to give their dears,
224          Pins and poking-sticks of steel,
What maids lack from head to heel.
Come buy of me, come ; come buy, come buy.
Buy, lads, or else your lasses cry.
Come buy.

CLOWN If I were not in love with Mopsa, thou shouldst
take no money of me ; but being enthralled as I am, it
will also be the bondage of certain ribbons and gloves.

MOPSA I was promised them against the feast, but they
come not too late now.

DORCAS He hath promised you more than that, or there
be liars.

MOPSA He hath paid you all he promised you. May be he
237 has paid you more, which will shame you to give him
again.

CLOWN Is there no manners left among maids ? Will they
wear their plackets where they should bear their faces ?
Is there not milking-time, when you are going to bed, or
242 kiln-hole, to whistle off these secrets, but you must be
tittle-tattling before all our guests ? 'Tis well they are

---

213 *You have* there are some   217 *Cyprus* cloth from Cyprus   220 *Bugle*
bead   222 *quoifs* coifs, head-dresses   224 *poking-sticks* metal rods used to
iron pleats   237–38 *to give him again* into giving back to him   242 *kiln-hole*
fireplace

whispering. Clamor your tongues, and not a word more.  244

MOPSA  I have done. Come, you promised me a tawdry-  245
lace and a pair of sweet gloves.

CLOWN  Have I not told thee how I was cozened by the  247
way and lost all my money?

AUTOLYCUS  And indeed, sir, there are cozeners abroad;
therefore it behoves men to be wary.

CLOWN  Fear not thou, man; thou shalt lose nothing here.

AUTOLYCUS  I hope so, sir, for I have about me many
parcels of charge.                                        253

CLOWN  What hast here? Ballads?

MOPSA  Pray now, buy some. I love a ballad in print, a life,  255
for then we are sure they are true.

AUTOLYCUS  Here's one to a very doleful tune, how a
usurer's wife was brought to bed of twenty money-bags
at a burthen, and how she longed to eat adders' heads
and toads carbonadoed.                                    260

MOPSA  Is it true, think you?

AUTOLYCUS  Very true, and but a month old.

DORCAS  Bless me from marrying a usurer!

AUTOLYCUS  Here's the midwife's name to't, one Mistress
Tale-porter, and five or six honest wives that were
present. Why should I carry lies abroad?

MOPSA  Pray you now, buy it.

CLOWN  Come on, lay it by. And let's first see moe
ballads; we'll buy the other things anon.

AUTOLYCUS  Here's another ballad of a fish that appeared
upon the coast on Wednesday the fourscore of April,  271
forty thousand fathom above water, and sung this ballad
against the hard hearts of maids. It was thought she was
a woman and was turned into a cold fish for she would

---

244 *Clamor* stop (?) (It is said to be a technical term of bell-ringing, meaning
speed up and stop. Suggested emendations are 'clammer' and, recently by
Professor Sisson, 'clam a.')  245 *tawdry-lace* colored neckerchief  247
*cozened* cheated  253 *charge* value  255 *a life* on my life  260 *carbonadoed*
grilled  271–72 *fourscore . . . water* (parody of the kind of 'wonders'
narrated in broadside ballads)

not exchange flesh with one that loved her. The ballad
is very pitiful and as true.

DORCAS  Is it true too, think you?

AUTOLYCUS  Five justices' hands at it, and witnesses
more than my pack will hold.

CLOWN  Lay it by too. Another.

AUTOLUCUS  This is a merry ballad, but a very pretty one.

MOPSA  Let's have some merry ones.

AUTOLYCUS  Why, this is a passing merry one and goes to
the tune of 'Two maids wooing a man.' There's scarce a
285  maid westward but she sings it. 'Tis in request, I can
tell you.

MOPSA  We can both sing it; if thou'lt bear a part, thou
shalt hear. 'Tis in three parts.

DORCAS  We had the tune on't a month ago.

AUTOLYCUS  I can bear my part; you must know 'tis my
occupation. Have at it with you.

*Song.*

AUTOLYCUS  Get you hence, for I must go
        Where it fits not you to know.

DORCAS       Whither?

MOPSA           O, whither?

DORCAS              Whither?

MOPSA  It becomes thy oath full well,
        Thou to me thy secrets tell.

DORCAS       Me too; let me go thither.

298 MOPSA  Or thou goest to th' grange or mill.

DORCAS  If to either, thou dost ill.

AUTOLYCUS     Neither.

DORCAS          What, neither?

AUTOLYCUS              Neither.

DORCAS  Thou hast sworn my love to be.

MOPSA  Thou hast sworn it more to me.
        Then whither goest? say, whither?

**285** *westward* (in England the 'unspoiled' country)   **298** *grange* farm

94

CLOWN We'll have this song out anon by ourselves. My
father and the gentlemen are in sad talk, and we'll not 305
trouble them. Come, bring away thy pack after me.
Wenches, I'll buy for you both. Pedlar, let's have the
first choice. Follow me, girls.
                                      *[Exit with Dorcas and Mopsa.]*
AUTOLYCUS And you shall pay well for 'em.
    *[Follows singing.]*

                        *Song.*

        Will you buy any tape,
        Or lace for your cape,
        My dainty duck, my dear-a?
            Any silk, any thread,
            Any toys for your head
        Of the new'st and fin'st, fin'st wear-a?
            Come to the pedlar.
            Money's a meddler
        That doth utter all men's ware-a.     *Exit.* 318

    *[Enter Servant.]*
SERVANT Master, there is three carters, three shepherds,
three neatherds, three swineherds, that have made them- 320
selves all men of hair. They call themselves Saltiers, and 321
they have a dance which the wenches say is a gallimaufry 322
of gambols, because they are not in't; but they themselves are o' th' mind, if it be not too rough for some
that know little but bowling, it will please plentifully.
SHEPHERD Away! we'll none on't. Here has been too
much homely foolery already. I know, sir, we weary you. 327
POLIXENES You weary those that refresh us. Pray, let's
see these four threes of herdsmen.
SERVANT One three of them, by their own report, sir, 330
hath danced before the king; and not the worst of the

---

305 *sad* serious   318 *utter* sell   320 *neatherds* cowherds   321 *of hair* i.e.
wearing skins of animals; *Saltiers* i.e. satyrs   322 *gallimaufry* hodgepodge
327 *homely* lacking refinement   330 *One three* one group of three

332   three but jumps twelve foot and a half by th' squire.

SHEPHERD Leave your prating. Since these good men
are pleased, let them come in; but quickly now.

SERVANT Why, they stay at door, sir.     [*Exit.*]

   *Here a dance of twelve Satyrs.*

POLIXENES
O, father, you'll know more of that hereafter.
   [*To Camillo*]
Is it not too far gone? 'Tis time to part them.
He's simple and tells much. – How now, fair shepherd,
Your heart is full of something that does take
Your mind from feasting. Sooth, when I was young

341   And handed love as you do, I was wont
To load my she with knacks. I would have ransacked
The pedlar's silken treasury and have poured it
To her acceptance. You have let him go

345   And nothing marted with him. If your lass
Interpretation should abuse and call this

347   Your lack of love or bounty, you were straited

348   For a reply, at least if you make a care
Of happy holding her.

FLORIZEL          Old sir, I know
She prizes not such trifles as these are.
The gifts she looks from me are packed and locked
Up in my heart, which I have given already,

353   But not delivered. O, hear me breathe my life
Before this ancient sir, who, it should seem,
Hath sometime loved. I take thy hand, this hand
As soft as dove's down and as white as it,

357   Or Ethiopian's tooth, or the fanned snow that's bolted
By th' northern blasts twice o'er.

POLIXENES          What follows this?
How prettily the young swain seems to wash

---

332 *squire* square (cf. T-square)  341 *handed* pledged by the hand  345
*marted* traded  347 *straited* hard pressed  348 *care* serious wish  353
*breathe...life* vow  357 *fanned* blown; *bolted* sifted

The hand was fair before! I have put you out.
But to your protestation; let me hear
What you profess.

FLORIZEL          Do, and be witness to't.

POLIXENES
And this my neighbor too?

FLORIZEL          And he, and more
Than he, and men, the earth, the heavens, and all —
That, were I crowned the most imperial monarch,
Thereof most worthy, were I the fairest youth
That ever made eye swerve, had force and knowledge
More than was ever man's, I would not prize them
Without her love; for her employ them all;
Commend them and condemn them to her service     370
Or to their own perdition.

POLIXENES          Fairly offered.

CAMILLO
This shows a sound affection.

SHEPHERD          But, my daughter,
Say you the like to him?

PERDITA          I cannot speak
So well, nothing so well; no, nor mean better.
By th' pattern of mine own thoughts I cut out
The purity of his.

SHEPHERD          Take hands, a bargain!
And, friends unknown, you shall bear witness to't.
I give my daughter to him and will make
Her portion equal his.

FLORIZEL          O, that must be
I' th' virtue of your daughter. One being dead,
I shall have more than you can dream of yet,
Enough then for your wonder. But, come on,
Contract us 'fore these witnesses.

SHEPHERD          Come, your hand;
And, daughter, yours.

370 *condemn* (i.e. to *perdition*)

384 POLIXENES                Soft, swain, awhile, beseech you.
Have you a father?
FLORIZEL              I have, but what of him?
POLIXENES
Knows he of this?
FLORIZEL              He neither does nor shall.
POLIXENES
Methinks a father
Is at the nuptial of his son a guest
That best becomes the table. Pray you once more,
Is not your father grown incapable
391 Of reasonable affairs? Is he not stupid
With age and alt'ring rheums? Can he speak? hear?
393 Know man from man? dispute his own estate?
Lies he not bed-rid? and again does nothing
But what he did being childish?
FLORIZEL                          No, good sir,
He has his health and ampler strength indeed
Than most have of his age.
POLIXENES                      By my white beard,
You offer him, if this be so, a wrong
399 Something unfilial. Reason my son
Should choose himself a wife, but as good reason
The father, all whose joy is nothing else
But fair posterity, should hold some counsel
In such a business.
FLORIZEL              I yield all this;
But for some other reasons, my grave sir,
405 Which 'tis not fit you know, I not acquaint
My father of this business.
POLIXENES                      Let him know't.
FLORIZEL
He shall not.

---

384 *Soft* not so fast   391 *reasonable affairs* affairs requiring reason   393
*dispute* discuss   399 *Something* somewhat; *Reason* it is reasonable   405 *not*
i.e. can not

POLIXENES Prithee, let him.

FLORIZEL No, he must not.

SHEPHERD

Let him, my son. He shall not need to grieve
At knowing of thy choice.

FLORIZEL Come, come, he must not.
Mark our contract.

POLIXENES Mark your divorce, young sir,
[Discovers himself.]
Whom son I dare not call. Thou art too base
To be acknowledged. Thou a sceptre's heir,
That thus affects a sheep-hook! – Thou old traitor,
I am sorry that by hanging thee I can
But shorten thy life one week. – And thou, fresh piece
Of excellent witchcraft, who of force must know          416
The royal fool thou cop'st with –                        417

SHEPHERD O, my heart!

POLIXENES

I'll have thy beauty scratched with briers, and made
More homely than thy state. – For thee, fond boy,       419
If I may ever know thou dost but sigh
That thou no more shalt see this knack – as never       421
I mean thou shalt – we'll bar thee from succession,
Not hold thee of our blood – no, not our kin –
Farre than Deucalion off. Mark thou my words.           424
Follow us to the court. – Thou churl, for this time,
Though full of our displeasure, yet we free thee
From the dead blow of it. – And you, enchantment,       427
Worthy enough a herdsman – yea, him too,
That makes himself, but for our honor therein,
Unworthy thee – if ever henceforth thou
These rural latches to his entrance open,

---

416 *of force* perforce  417 *cop'st with* hast to do with  419 *fond* foolish
421 *knack* trifle  424 *Farre* farther; *Deucalion* (according to Greek myth-
ology this king of Thessaly and his wife were the only human beings to
escape a flood sent by Zeus)  427 *dead* death-dealing

Or hoop his body more with thy embraces,
I will devise a death as cruel for thee
434    As thou art tender to't.                   *Exit.*

PERDITA               Even here undone!
I was not much afeard; for once or twice
I was about to speak and tell him plainly
The selfsame sun that shines upon his court
Hides not his visage from our cottage but
Looks on alike. Will't please you, sir, be gone?
I told you what would come of this. Beseech you,
Of your own state take care. This dream of mine –
Being now awake, I'll queen it no inch farther,
But milk my ewes and weep.

CAMILLO               Why, how now, father?
Speak ere thou diest.

SHEPHERD          I cannot speak, nor think,
Nor dare to know that which I know. O sir,
You have undone a man of fourscore three,
That thought to fill his grave in quiet, yea,
448    To die upon the bed my father died,
To lie close by his honest bones; but now
Some hangman must put on my shroud and lay me
Where no priest shovels in dust. O cursèd wretch,
That knew'st this was the prince, and wouldst adventure
To mingle faith with him. Undone! undone!
If I might die within this hour, I have lived
To die when I desire.                 *Exit.*

FLORIZEL         Why look you so upon me?
I am but sorry, not afeard; delayed,
But nothing altered. What I was, I am,
458    More straining on for plucking back, not following
My leash unwillingly.

CAMILLO            Gracious my lord,
You know your father's temper. At this time
He will allow no speech, which I do guess

---

434 *tender* vulnerable  448 *died* i.e. died upon  458–59 *following . . . unwillingly* i.e. dragged along

You do not purpose to him; and as hardly
Will he endure your sight as yet, I fear.
Then, till the fury of his highness settle,
Come not before him.

FLORIZEL                    I not purpose it.
I think Camillo?

CAMILLO              Even he, my lord.

PERDITA
How often have I told you 'twould be thus?
How often said my dignity would last                    468
But till 'twere known!

FLORIZEL                    It cannot fail but by
The violation of my faith; and then
Let nature crush the sides o' th' earth together
And mar the seeds within. Lift up thy looks.
From my succession wipe me, father. I
Am heir to my affection.

CAMILLO                    Be advised.

FLORIZEL
I am, and by my fancy. If my reason                    475
Will thereto be obedient, I have reason;
If not, my senses, better pleased with madness,
Do bid it welcome.

CAMILLO              This is desperate, sir.

FLORIZEL
So call it, but it does fulfil my vow.
I needs must think it honesty. Camillo,
Not for Bohemia nor the pomp that may
Be thereat gleaned, for all the sun sees or
The close earth wombs or the profound seas hide    483
In unknown fathoms, will I break my oath
To this my fair beloved. Therefore, I pray you,
As you have ever been my father's honored friend,
When he shall miss me – as, in faith, I mean not
To see him any more – cast your good counsels

468 *dignity* i.e. honor of being the Prince's betrothed   475 *fancy* love
483 *wombs* encloses

Upon his passion. Let myself and fortune
490    Tug for the time to come. This you may know
And so deliver: I am put to sea
With her who here I cannot hold on shore.
And most opportune to our need I have
A vessel rides fast by, but not prepared
For this design. What course I mean to hold
496    Shall nothing benefit your knowledge, nor
Concern me the reporting.

CAMILLO                         O my lord,
I would your spirit were easier for advice
Or stronger for your need.

FLORIZEL                         Hark, Perdita.
        [Draws her aside.]
I'll hear you by and by.

CAMILLO                   He's irremovable,
Resolved for flight. Now were I happy if
His going I could frame to serve my turn,
Save him from danger, do him love and honor,
Purchase the sight again of dear Sicilia
And that unhappy king, my master, whom
I so much thirst to see.

FLORIZEL                   Now, good Camillo.
507    I am so fraught with curious business that
I leave out ceremony.

CAMILLO                   Sir, I think
You have heard of my poor services i' th' love
That I have borne your father?

FLORIZEL                         Very nobly
Have you deserved. It is my father's music
To speak your deeds, not little of his care
To have them recompensed as thought on.

CAMILLO                                        Well, my lord,
If you may please to think I love the king
And, through him, what's nearest to him, which is

490 *Tug* contend   496–97 *Shall . . . reporting* it does not behoove you to
know nor me to say   507 *curious* requiring care

Your gracious self, embrace but my direction.  516
If your more ponderous and settled project
May suffer alteration, on mine honor,
I'll point you where you shall have such receiving
As shall become your highness, where you may
Enjoy your mistress, from the whom, I see,
There's no disjunction to be made but by –
As heavens forfend! – your ruin; marry her,
And, with my best endeavors in your absence,
Your discontenting father strive to qualify  525
And bring him up to liking.

FLORIZEL                          How, Camillo,
May this, almost a miracle, be done?
That I may call thee something more than man,
And after that trust to thee.

CAMILLO                          Have you thought on
A place whereto you'll go?

FLORIZEL                          Not any yet.
But as th' unthought-on accident is guilty  531
To what we wildly do, so we profess
Ourselves to be the slaves of chance, and flies
Of every wind that blows.

CAMILLO                          Then list to me.
This follows: if you will not change your purpose
But undergo this flight, make for Sicilia,
And there present yourself and your fair princess,
For so I see she must be, 'fore Leontes.
She shall be habited as it becomes
The partner of your bed. Methinks I see
Leontes opening his free arms and weeping  541
His welcomes forth; asks thee the son forgiveness,
As 'twere i' th' father's person; kisses the hands
Of your fresh princess; o'er and o'er divides him
'Twixt his unkindness and his kindness; th' one

---

516 *embrace . . . direction* accept my advice  525 *qualify* assuage  531–32
*unthought-on . . . do* i.e. his unforeseen discovery by his father is to blame for
what he rashly does  541 *free* hospitable

He chides to hell and bids the other grow
Faster than thought or time.

FLORIZEL                          Worthy Camillo,
548   What color for my visitation shall I
Hold up before him?

CAMILLO                  Sent by the king your father
To greet him and to give him comforts. Sir,
The manner of your bearing towards him, with
What you, as from your father, shall deliver,
Things known betwixt us three, I'll write you down,
554   The which shall point you forth at every sitting
What you must say, that he shall not perceive
556   But that you have your father's bosom there
And speak his very heart.

FLORIZEL                          I am bound to you.
558   There is some sap in this.

CAMILLO                          A course more promising
Than a wild dedication of yourselves
To unpathed waters, undreamed shores, most certain
To miseries enough; no hope to help you,
But as you shake off one to take another;
Nothing so certain as your anchors, who
Do their best office if they can but stay you
Where you'll be loath to be. Besides, you know
Prosperity's the very bond of love,
Whose fresh complexion and whose heart together
Affliction alters.

PERDITA                  One of these is true.
I think affliction may subdue the cheek
570   But not take in the mind.

CAMILLO                          Yea, say you so?
571   There shall not at your father's house these seven years
Be born another such.

548 *color* pretext   554 *point . . . sitting* guide you at every interview   556
*bosom* confidence   558 *sap* element essential to life   570 *take in* subdue
571 *these seven years* i.e. for a long time to come ('seven' not to be taken
literally)

FLORIZEL                My good Camillo,
  She's as forward of her breeding as                    573
  She is i' th' rear 'our birth.                          574
CAMILLO                    I cannot say 'tis pity
  She lacks instructions, for she seems a mistress    575
  To most that teach.
PERDITA                Your pardon, sir. For this
  I'll blush you thanks.
FLORIZEL                My prettiest Perdita!
  But O, the thorns we stand upon! Camillo,
  Preserver of my father, now of me,
  The medicine of our house, how shall we do?
  We are not furnished like Bohemia's son,
  Nor shall appear in Sicilia.                          582
CAMILLO                My lord,
  Fear none of this. I think you know my fortunes
  Do all lie there. It shall be so my care
  To have you royally appointed as if
  The scene you play were mine. For instance, sir,
  That you may know you shall not want, one word.
    *[They talk aside.] Enter Autolycus.*
AUTOLYCUS Ha, ha, what a fool Honesty is! and Trust,
  his sworn brother, a very simple gentleman! I have sold
  all my trumpery. Not a counterfeit stone, not a ribbon,
  glass, pomander, brooch, table-book, ballad, knife, tape,    591
  glove, shoe-tie, bracelet, horn-ring, to keep my pack
  from fasting. They throng who should buy first, as if my
  trinkets had been hallowed and brought a benediction to
  the buyer; by which means I saw whose purse was best in    595
  picture, and what I saw, to my good use I remembered.
  My clown, who wants but something to be a reasonable
  man, grew so in love with the wenches' song that he
  would not stir his pettitoes till he had both tune and    599

---

573 *forward of* beyond   574 *'our* of our   575 *instructions* schooling   582
*appear* i.e. as the king's son   591 *table-book* note-book (cf. Hamlet's
tables)   595–96 *was best in picture* looked best   599 *pettitoes* toes (usually
of a pig)

words, which so drew the rest of the herd to me that all
601 their other senses stuck in ears. You might have pinched
602 a placket, it was senseless; 'twas nothing to geld a cod-
piece of a purse; I would have filed keys off that hung in
604 chains. No hearing, no feeling, but my sir's song and admiring the nothing of it. So that in this time of lethargy I
picked and cut most of their festival purses; and had not
the old man come in with a whoo-bub against his daugh-
608 ter and the king's son and scared my choughs from the
chaff, I had not left a purse alive in the whole army.

*[Camillo, Florizel, and Perdita come forward.]*

CAMILLO
Nay, but my letters, by this means being there
So soon as you arrive, shall clear that doubt.

FLORIZEL
And those that you'll procure from King Leontes –

CAMILLO
Shall satisfy your father.

PERDITA                        Happy be you!
All that you speak shows fair.

CAMILLO *[seeing Autolycus]*    Who have we here?
615 We'll make an instrument of this, omit
Nothing may give us aid.

AUTOLYCUS If they have overheard me now, why, hanging.

CAMILLO
How now, good fellow? Why shak'st thou so?
Fear not, man; here's no harm intended to thee.

AUTOLYCUS I am a poor fellow, sir.

CAMILLO Why, be so still; here's nobody will steal that
622 from thee. Yet for the outside of thy poverty we must
623 make an exchange. Therefore discase thee instantly –

---

601 *stuck in ears* were devoted to listening   602 *senseless* without feeling
602–03 *geld . . . purse* remove a purse from a pocket   604 *my sir's* i.e. the
clown's   608 *choughs* birds of the crow family   615 *instrument* means to
an end   622 *the outside . . . poverty* thy rags   623 *discase* undress

thou must think there's a necessity in't – and change
garments with this gentleman. Though the pennyworth 625
on his side be the worst, yet hold thee, there's some boot. 626

AUTOLYCUS I am a poor fellow, sir. *[aside]* I know ye
well enough.

CAMILLO Nay, prithee, dispatch. The gentleman is half 629
flayed already. 630

AUTOLYCUS Are you in earnest, sir? *[aside]* I smell the
trick on't.

FLORIZEL Dispatch, I prithee.

AUTOLYCUS Indeed, I have had earnest, but I cannot 634
with conscience take it.

CAMILLO Unbuckle, unbuckle.
          *[Florizel and Autolycus exchange garments.]*
Fortunate mistress – let my prophecy
Come home to ye! – you must retire yourself 638
Into some covert. Take your sweetheart's hat
And pluck it o'er your brows, muffle your face,
Dismantle you, and, as you can, disliken 641
The truth of your own seeming, that you may –
For I do fear eyes over – to shipboard 643
Get undescried.

PERDITA          I see the play so lies
That I must bear a part.

CAMILLO          No remedy.
Have you done there?

FLORIZEL          Should I now meet my father,
He would not call me son.

CAMILLO          Nay, you shall have no hat.
          *[Gives it to Perdita.]*
Come, lady, come. Farewell, my friend.

AUTOLYCUS          Adieu, sir.

---

625–26 *Though . . . worst* though he gets the worse in the exchange  626 *boot*
i.e. something additional (usually to equalize an exchange)  629 *dispatch*
make haste  630 *flayed* skinned  634 *earnest* partial prepayment  638
*Come . . . ye* be fulfilled  641–42 *as . . . seeming* as far as you can, alter your
true appearance  643 *eyes over* spying

FLORIZEL
O Perdita, what have we twain forgot?
Pray you, a word.

CAMILLO [aside]
What I do next, shall be to tell the king
Of this escape and whither they are bound;
Wherein my hope is I shall so prevail
To force him after; in whose company
I shall review Sicilia, for whose sight
656   I have a woman's longing.

FLORIZEL                          Fortune speed us!
Thus we set on, Camillo, to the seaside.

CAMILLO
The swifter speed the better.

> *Exeunt [Florizel, Perdita, and Camillo].*

AUTOLYCUS I understand the business, I hear it. To have
an open ear, a quick eye, and a nimble hand is necessary
for a cutpurse. A good nose is requisite also, to smell out
work for the other senses. I see this is the time that the
unjust man doth thrive. What an exchange had this been
without boot! What a boot is here with this exchange!
Sure the gods do this year connive at us, and we may do
any thing extempore. The prince himself is about a
piece of iniquity, stealing away from his father with his
667   clog at his heels. If I thought it were a piece of honesty
to acquaint the king withal, I would not do't. I hold it
the more knavery to conceal it, and therein am I
constant to my profession.

> *Enter Clown and Shepherd.*

Aside, aside! Here is more matter for a hot brain. Every
lane's end, every shop, church, session, hanging, yields
a careful man work.

CLOWN See, see! What a man you are now! There is no

656 *longing* (as for particular foods during pregnancy)   667 *clog* (anything
which impedes movement)

other way but to tell the king she's a changeling and 676
none of your flesh and blood.

SHEPHERD Nay, but hear me.

CLOWN Nay, but hear me.

SHEPHERD Go to, then. 680

CLOWN She being none of your flesh and blood, your
flesh and blood has not offended the king, and so your
flesh and blood is not to be punished by him. Show
those things you found about her, those secret things,
all but what she has with her. This being done, let the
law go whistle, I warrant you.

SHEPHERD I will tell the king all, every word – yea, and
his son's pranks too, who, I may say, is no honest man,
neither to his father nor to me, to go about to make me
the king's brother-in-law.

CLOWN Indeed, brother-in-law was the farthest off you
could have been to him, and then your blood had been
the dearer by I know how much an ounce. 693

AUTOLYCUS [aside] Very wisely, puppies.

SHEPHERD Well, let us to the king. There is that in this
fardel will make him scratch his beard. 696

AUTOLYCUS [aside] I know not what impediment this
complaint may be to the flight of my master.

CLOWN Pray heartily he be at' palace. 699

AUTOLYCUS [aside] Though I am not naturally honest, I
am so sometimes by chance. Let me pocket up my
pedlar's excrement. [Takes off his false beard.] How 702
now, rustics, whither are you bound?

SHEPHERD To the palace, an it like your worship. 704

AUTOLYCUS Your affairs there, what, with whom, the
condition of that fardel, the place of your dwelling,
your names, your ages, of what having, breeding, and 707
anything that is fitting to be known, discover. 708

676 *changeling* a child left (by fairies) with other than its true parents  680
*Go to* go on  693 *the dearer* of greater worth  696 *fardel* bundle  699 *at'*
at the  702 *excrement* appendage  704 *an it like* if it please  707 *having*
property  708 *discover* reveal

CLOWN We are but plain fellows, sir.

AUTOLYCUS A lie! You are rough and hairy. Let me have
no lying. It becomes none but tradesmen, and they often
give us soldiers the lie; but we pay them for it with
stamped coin, not stabbing steel; therefore they do not
give us the lie.

CLOWN Your worship had like to have given us one, if
716    you had not taken yourself with the manner.

SHEPHERD Are you a courtier, an't like you, sir?

AUTOLYCUS Whether it like me or no, I am a courtier.
719    Seest thou not the air of the court in these enfoldings?
Hath not my gait in it the measure of the court?
Receives not thy nose court-odor from me? Reflect I
not on thy baseness, court-contempt? Thinkest thou,
723    for that I insinuate, or toaze from thee thy business, I
724    am therefore no courtier? I am courtier cap-a-pe, and
one that will either push on or pluck back thy business
there. Whereupon I command thee to open thy affair.

SHEPHERD My business, sir, is to the king.

AUTOLYCUS What advocate hast thou to him?

SHEPHERD I know not, an't like you.

730    CLOWN Advocate 's the court-word for a pheasant. Say
you have none.

SHEPHERD None, sir. I have no pheasant, cock nor hen.

AUTOLYCUS
How blessèd are we that are not simple men!
Yet nature might have made me as these are;
Therefore I will not disdain.

CLOWN This cannot be but a great courtier.

SHEPHERD His garments are rich, but he wears them not
handsomely.

CLOWN He seems to be the more noble in being fantasti-
740    cal. A great man, I'll warrant. I know by the picking on's
teeth.

**716** *taken . . . manner* caught yourself in the act (?)    **719** *enfoldings* clothes
**723** *toaze* tear    **724** *cap-a-pe* from head to foot    **730** *pheasant* i.e. as a bribe
to the judge (the clown confuses the two kinds of courts)    **740–41** *picking
on's teeth* (picking the teeth was an affectation of would-be gallants)

AUTOLYCUS The fardel there? What's i' the fardel?
Wherefore that box?

SHEPHERD Sir, there lies such secrets in this fardel and
box, which none must know but the king, and which he
shall know within this hour if I may come to the speech
of him.

AUTOLYCUS Age, thou hast lost thy labor.    748

SHEPHERD Why, sir?

AUTOLYCUS The king is not at the palace. He is gone
aboard a new ship to purge melancholy and air himself,
for, if thou be'st capable of things serious, thou must
know the king is full of grief.

SHEPHERD So 'tis said, sir – about his son, that should
have married a shepherd's daughter.

AUTOLYCUS If that shepherd be not in hand-fast, let him 756
fly. The curses he shall have, the tortures he shall feel,
will break the back of man, the heart of monster.

CLOWN Think you so, sir?

AUTOLYCUS Not he alone shall suffer what wit can make
heavy and vengeance bitter; but those that are germane
to him, though removed fifty times, shall all come under
the hangman, which, though it be great pity, yet it is
necessary. An old sheep-whistling rogue, a ram-tender,
to offer to have his daughter come into grace! Some say 765
he shall be stoned, but that death is too soft for him, say
I. Draw our throne into a sheep-cote! All deaths are too
few, the sharpest too easy.

CLOWN Has the old man e'er a son, sir, do you hear, an't
like you, sir?

AUTOLYCUS He has a son, who shall be flayed alive; then
'nointed over with honey, set on the head of a wasp's
nest; then stand till he be three quarters and a dram
dead; then recovered again with aqua-vitae or some 774
other hot infusion. Then, raw as he is, and in the hottest

---

748 *Age* old man   756 *hand-fast* custody   765 *grace* honor   774 *aqua-vitae*
brandy

776  day prognostication proclaims, shall he be set against a
brick-wall, the sun looking with a southward eye upon
him, where he is to behold him with flies blown to death.
But what talk we of these traitorly rascals, whose miseries are to be smiled at, their offenses being so capital?
Tell me, for you seem to be honest plain men, what you
782  have to the king. Being something gently considered,
I'll bring you where he is aboard, tender your persons to
his presence, whisper him in your behalfs; and if it be in
man besides the king to effect your suits, here is man
shall do it.

786  CLOWN  He seems to be of great authority. Close with him,
give him gold; and though authority be a stubborn bear,
yet he is oft led by the nose with gold. Show the inside of
your purse to the outside of his hand, and no more ado.
Remember 'stoned,' and 'flayed alive.'

SHEPHERD  An't please you, sir, to undertake the business for us, here is that gold I have. I'll make it as much
more and leave this young man in pawn till I bring it
you.

AUTOLYCUS  After I have done what I promised?

SHEPHERD  Ay, sir.

796  AUTOLYCUS  Well, give me the moiety. Are you a party
in this business?

798  CLOWN  In some sort, sir. But though my case be a pitiful
one, I hope I shall not be flayed out of it.

AUTOLYCUS  O, that's the case of the shepherd's son.
Hang him, he'll be made an example.

CLOWN  Comfort, good comfort! We must to the king
and show our strange sights. He must know 'tis none of
804  your daughter nor my sister; we are gone else. Sir, I
will give you as much as this old man does when the

---

776 *prognostication* forecast (forecasts for the coming year were published
annually)   782 *something . . . considered* given some consideration, i.e. bribe
786 *Close* come to an agreement   796 *moiety* half   798 *case* (1) position *in
this business*, (2) skin   804 *gone* undone

business is performed, and remain, as he says, your
pawn till it be brought you.

AUTOLYCUS I will trust you. Walk before toward the
seaside. Go on the right hand. I will but look upon the
hedge and follow you.

CLOWN We are blest in this man, as I may say, even blest.

SHEPHERD Let's before as he bids us. He was provided
to do us good.          *[Exeunt Shepherd and Clown.]*

AUTOLYCUS If I had a mind to be honest, I see Fortune
would not suffer me; she drops booties in my mouth. I
am courted now with a double occasion, gold and a       816
means to do the prince my master good, which who
knows how that may turn back to my advancement? I      818
will bring these two moles, these blind ones, aboard him.  819
If he think it fit to shore them again and that the complaint they have to the king concerns him nothing, let
him call me rogue for being so far officious, for I am
proof against that title and what shame else belongs to't.
To him will I present them; there may be matter in it.
                                          *Exit.*

\*

*Enter Leontes, Cleomenes, Dion, Paulina, Servants.*    V, i

CLEOMENES
Sir, you have done enough, and have performed
A saint-like sorrow. No fault could you make
Which you have not redeemed – indeed, paid down
More penitence than done trespass. At the last,
Do as the heavens have done, forget your evil;          5
With them forgive yourself.

LEONTES                        Whilst I remember
Her and her virtues, I cannot forget
My blemishes in them, and so still think of             8
The wrong I did myself, which was so much

---

816 *courted . . . with* tempted . . . by   818 *turn back* revert   819 *aboard him*
to him aboard (the ship)
V, i The palace of Leontes   5 *evil* sin   8 *in* i.e. in relation to

That heirless it hath made my kingdom and
Destroyed the sweet'st companion that e'er man
Bred his hopes out of.

PAULINA                    True, too true, my lord.
If one by one you wedded all the world,
Or from the all that are took something good
To make a perfect woman, she you killed
Would be unparalleled.

LEONTES                    I think so. Killed?
She I killed? I did so, but thou strik'st me
Sorely to say I did. It is as bitter
19    Upon thy tongue as in my thought. Now, good now,
Say so but seldom.

CLEOMENES                    Not at all, good lady.
You might have spoken a thousand things that would
22    Have done the time more benefit and graced
Your kindness better.

PAULINA                    You are one of those
Would have him wed again.

DION                    If you would not so,
You pity not the state nor the remembrance
Of his most sovereign name, consider little
What dangers, by his highness' fail of issue,
May drop upon his kingdom and devour
29    Incertain lookers on. What were more holy
Than to rejoice the former queen is well?
What holier than, for royalty's repair,
For present comfort and for future good,
To bless the bed of majesty again
With a sweet fellow to't?

PAULINA                    There is none worthy,
Respecting her that's gone. Besides, the gods
Will have fulfilled their secret purposes;
For has not the divine Apollo said,
Is't not the tenor of his oracle,

19 *good now* i.e. I pray you (?) (cf. *Hamlet* I, i, 70)   22 *graced* befitted   29
*Incertain* confused (as to an heir to the throne)

That King Leontes shall not have an heir
Till his lost child be found? Which that it shall
Is all as monstrous to our human reason                    41
As my Antigonus to break his grave
And come again to me, who, on my life,
Did perish with the infant. 'Tis your counsel
My lord should to the heavens be contrary,
Oppose against their wills.
    *[To Leontes]*          Care not for issue;
The crown will find an heir. Great Alexander
Left his to th' worthiest; so his successor
Was like to be the best.
LEONTES                    Good Paulina,
Who hast the memory of Hermione,
I know, in honor, O that ever I
Had squared me to thy counsel! Then even now    52
I might have looked upon my queen's full eyes,
Have taken treasure from her lips—
PAULINA                    And left them
More rich for what they yielded.
LEONTES                    Thou speak'st truth.
No more such wives; therefore, no wife! One worse,    56
And better used, would make her sainted spirit
Again possess her corpse, and on this stage
(Where we offenders now) appear soul-vexed,    59
And begin, 'Why to me?'
PAULINA                    Had she such power,
She had just cause.
LEONTES          She had, and would incense me
To murder her I married.
PAULINA          I should so.
Were I the ghost that walked, I'ld bid you mark
Her eye, and tell me for what dull part in't
You chose her. Then I'ld shriek, that even your ears

41 *monstrous* incredible   52 *squarred me to* acted in accordance with   56
*No more* there are no more   59 *now* now play our parts (? an obscure
passage)

Should rift to hear me, and the words that followed
Should be 'Remember mine.'

LEONTES                      Stars, stars,
And all eyes else dead coals! Fear thou no wife;
I'll have no wife, Paulina.

PAULINA                   Will you swear
Never to marry but by my free leave?

LEONTES
Never, Paulina, so be blest my spirit.

PAULINA
Then, good my lords, bear witness to his oath.

CLEOMENES
73  You tempt him overmuch.

PAULINA                 Unless another,
As like Hermione as is her picture,
75  Affront his eye.

CLEOMENES      Good madam –

PAULINA                  I have done.
Yet, if my lord will marry – if you will, sir,
No remedy but you will – give me the office
To choose you a queen. She shall not be so young
As was your former, but she shall be such
As, walked your first queen's ghost, it should take joy
To see her in your arms.

LEONTES             My true Paulina,
We shall not marry till thou bid'st us.

PAULINA                That
83  Shall be when your first queen's again in breath.
Never till then.

      *Enter a Servant.*

SERVANT
One that gives out himself Prince Florizel,
Son of Polixenes, with his princess – she
The fairest I have yet beheld – desires access
To your high presence.

73 *tempt* urge   75 *Affront* confront   83 *in breath* alive

LEONTES                    What with him? He comes not
    Like to his father's greatness. His approach,                    89
    So out of circumstance and sudden, tells us                      90
    'Tis not a visitation framed, but forced                         91
    By need and accident. What train?
SERVANT                              But few,
    And those but mean.
LEONTES                    His princess, say you, with him?
SERVANT
    Ay, the most peerless piece of earth, I think,
    That e'er the sun shone bright on.
PAULINA                              O Hermione.
    As every present time doth boast itself
    Above a better gone, so must thy grave
    Give way to what's seen now. Sir, you yourself
    Have said and writ so, but your writing now
    Is colder than that theme. She had not been,               100
    Nor was not to be equalled – thus your verse
    Flowed with her beauty once. 'Tis shrewdly ebbed
    To say you have seen a better.
SERVANT                    Pardon, madam.
    The one I have almost forgot – your pardon;
    The other, when she has obtained your eye,
    Will have your tongue too. This is a creature,
    Would she begin a sect, might quench the zeal
    Of all professors else, make proselytes                    108
    Of who she but bid follow.
PAULINA                    How? not women?
SERVANT
    Women will love her that she is a woman
    More worth than any man; men, that she is
    The rarest of all women.
LEONTES                    Go, Cleomenes.
    Yourself, assisted with your honored friends,

---

**89** *approach* coming   **90** *out of circumstance* without formality   **91** *framed*
premeditated   **100** *colder* i.e. more dead   **108** *professors else* those who
profess other faiths

Bring them to our embracement.

> *Exit [Cleomenes with others].*
>                                    Still, 'tis strange

115      He thus should steal upon us.

PAULINA                 Had our prince,
Jewel of children, seen this hour, he had paired
Well with this lord. There was not full a month
Between their births.

LEONTES           Prithee, no more; cease. Thou know'st
He dies to me again when talked of. Sure,
When I shall see this gentleman, thy speeches
Will bring me to consider that which may

122      Unfurnish me of reason. They are come.

> *Enter Florizel, Perdita, Cleomenes, and others.*

Your mother was most true to wedlock, prince,
For she did print your royal father off,
Conceiving you. Were I but twenty-one,
Your father's image is so hit in you,
His very air, that I should call you brother,
As I did him, and speak of something wildly
By us performed before. Most dearly welcome!
And your fair princess – goddess! O, alas!
I lost a couple that 'twixt heaven and earth
Might thus have stood begetting wonder as
You, gracious couple, do. And then I lost –
All mine own folly – the society,
Amity too, of your brave father, whom,
Though bearing misery, I desire my life
Once more to look on him.

FLORIZEL          By his command
Have I here touched Sicilia, and from him

139      Give you all greetings that a king, at friend,
Can send his brother; and, but infirmity

141      Which waits upon worn times hath something seized

---

115 *steal . . . us* i.e. come unannounced    122 *Unfurnish* deprive    139 *at friend* in friendship    141 *waits . . . times* accompanies old age; *something seized* somewhat taken away

His wished ability, he had himself
The lands and waters 'twixt your throne and his
Measured to look upon you, whom he loves –                    144
He bade me say so – more than all the sceptres
And those that bear them living.

LEONTES                                O my brother,
Good gentleman, the wrongs I have done thee stir
Afresh within me, and these thy offices,                    148
So rarely kind, are as interpreters                    149
Of my behindhand slackness. Welcome hither,
As is the spring to th' earth. And hath he too
Exposed this paragon to th' fearful usage,
At least ungentle, of the dreadful Neptune,
To greet a man not worth her pains, much less
Th' adventure of her person?                    155

FLORIZEL                                Good my lord,
She came from Libya.

LEONTES                    Where the warlike Smalus,
That noble honored lord, is feared and loved?

FLORIZEL
Most royal sir, from thence, from him, whose daughter
His tears proclaimed his, parting with her. Thence,
A prosperous south-wind friendly, we have crossed,
To execute the charge my father gave me
For visiting your highness. My best train
I have from your Sicilian shores dismissed,
Who for Bohemia bend, to signify
Not only my success in Libya, sir,
But my arrival and my wife's in safety
Here where we are.

LEONTES                    The blessèd gods
Purge all infection from our air whilst you
Do climate here! You have a holy father,                    169
A graceful gentleman, against whose person,                    170

144 *Measured* journeyed over  148 *offices* courtesies  149–50 *are . . . slackness* emphasize my tardy, inadequate action  155 *adventure* risk
169 *climate* dwell  170 *graceful* gracious

So sacred as it is, I have done sin,
For which the heavens, taking angry note,
Have left me issueless ; and your father's blest,
As he from heaven merits it, with you,
Worthy his goodness. What might I have been,
Might I a son and daughter now have looked on,
Such goodly things as you ?

*Enter a Lord.*

LORD                              Most noble sir,
That which I shall report will bear no credit,
Were not the proof so nigh. Please you, great sir,
Bohemia greets you from himself by me,

181    Desires you to attach his son, who has –
His dignity and duty both cast off –
Fled from his father, from his hopes, and with
A shepherd's daughter.

LEONTES                   Where's Bohemia ? Speak.

LORD
Here in your city. I now came from him.

186    I speak amazedly, and it becomes
My marvel and my message. To your court

188    Whiles he was hast'ning – in the chase, it seems,
Of this fair couple – meets he on the way
The father of this seeming lady and
Her brother, having both their country quitted
With this young prince.

FLORIZEL               Camillo has betrayed me,
Whose honor and whose honesty till now
Endured all weathers.

LORD                   Lay't so to his charge.
He's with the king your father.

LEONTES                        Who ? Camillo ?

LORD
Camillo, sir. I spake with him, who now
Has these poor men in question. Never saw I

181 *attach* arrest   186 *amazedly* confusedly   186–87 *it . . . marvel* my
confused speech suits (results from) my wonder   188 *chase* pursuit

Wretches so quake. They kneel, they kiss the earth,
Forswear themselves as often as they speak.
Bohemia stops his ears, and threatens them
With divers deaths in death.                                      201

PERDITA                         O my poor father!
The heaven sets spies upon us, will not have
Our contract celebrated.

LEONTES                          You are married?

FLORIZEL
We are not, sir, nor are we like to be.
The stars, I see, will kiss the valleys first;
The odds for high and low's alike.                               206

LEONTES                              My lord,
Is this the daughter of a king?

FLORIZEL                          She is
When once she is my wife.

LEONTES
That 'once,' I see by your good father's speed,
Will come on very slowly. I am sorry,
Most sorry, you have broken from his liking
Where you were tied in duty, and as sorry
Your choice is not so rich in worth as beauty,                   213
That you might well enjoy her.

FLORIZEL                         Dear, look up.
Though Fortune, visible an enemy,                                215
Should chase us with my father, power no jot
Hath she to change our loves. Beseech you, sir,
Remember since you owed no more to time                          218
Than I do now. With thought of such affections,
Step forth mine advocate. At your request
My father will grant precious things as trifles.

LEONTES
Would he do so, I'ld beg your precious mistress,
Which he counts but a trifle.

201 *deaths in death* tortures   206 *odds . . . alike* high and low are alike
subject to misfortune   213 *worth* high birth   215 *visible* clearly   **218-19**
*since . . . now* when you were my age

PAULINA                          Sir, my liege,
Your eye hath too much youth in't. Not a month
'Fore your queen died, she was more worth such gazes
Than what you look on now.

LEONTES                     I thought of her
Even in these looks I made. *[to Florizel]* But your petition
Is yet unanswered. I will to your father.

229   Your honor not o'erthrown by your desires,
I am friend to them and you. Upon which errand
I now go toward him; therefore follow me

232   And mark what way I make. Come, good my lord.

                                   *Exeunt.*

                     *

V, ii          *Enter Autolycus and a Gentleman.*

AUTOLYCUS  Beseech you, sir, were you present at this
relation?

1. GENTLEMAN  I was by at the opening of the fardel,
heard the old shepherd deliver the manner how he
found it; whereupon, after a little amazedness, we were
all commanded out of the chamber. Only this methought I heard the shepherd say, he found the child.

AUTOLYCUS  I would most gladly know the issue of it.

9   1. GENTLEMAN  I make a broken delivery of the business;
but the changes I perceived in the king and Camillo

11   were very notes of admiration. They seemed almost,
with staring on one another, to tear the cases of their
eyes. There was speech in their dumbness, language in
their very gesture. They looked as they had heard of a

15   world ransomed, or one destroyed. A notable passion of
wonder appeared in them. But the wisest beholder, that

17   knew no more but seeing, could not say if the impor-

---

229 *Your . . . desires* if your desires have not led you to do what is dis-
honorable   232 *way* progress
V, ii An open place near the palace of Leontes   9 *make . . . delivery* give
a fragmentary account   11 *admiration* wonder   15 *passion* emotion   17
*seeing* what he saw; *importance* import

tance were joy or sorrow; but in the extremity of the
one, it must needs be.

*Enter another Gentleman.*

Here comes a gentleman that haply knows more. The 20
news, Rogero?

2. GENTLEMAN Nothing but bonfires. The oracle is fulfilled; the king's daughter is found. Such a deal of
wonder is broken out within this hour that ballad-
makers cannot be able to express it.

*Enter another Gentleman.*

Here comes the Lady Paulina's steward; he can deliver 26
you more. How goes it now, sir? This news which is
called true is so like an old tale that the verity of it is in
strong suspicion. Has the king found his heir?

3. GENTLEMAN Most true, if ever truth were pregnant 30
by circumstance. That which you hear you'll swear you
see, there is such unity in the proofs. The mantle of 32
Queen Hermione's, her jewel about the neck of it, the
letters of Antigonus found with it, which they know to
be his character, the majesty of the creature in resem- 35
blance of the mother, the affection of nobleness which 36
nature shows above her breeding, and many other evi-
dences proclaim her with all certainty to be the king's
daughter. Did you see the meeting of the two kings?

2. GENTLEMAN No.

3. GENTLEMAN Then have you lost a sight which was to
be seen, cannot be spoken of. There might you have beheld one joy crown another, so and in such manner that
it seemed sorrow wept to take leave of them, for their joy
waded in tears. There was casting up of eyes, holding up
of hands, with countenance of such distraction that they
were to be known by garment, not by favor. Our king, 47
being ready to leap out of himself for joy of his found
daughter, as if that joy were now become a loss, cries, 'O,

20 *haply* perhaps   26 *deliver* tell   30–31 *pregnant by circumstance* obvious
from the evidence   32 *unity* agreement   35 *character* handwriting   36
*affection of* natural tendency toward   47 *favor* features

123

thy mother, thy mother!' then asks Bohemia forgiveness; then embraces his son-in-law; then again worries
52 he his daughter with clipping her; now he thanks the old
53 shepherd, which stands by like a weather-bitten conduit
of many kings' reigns. I never heard of such another en-
55 counter, which lames report to follow it and undoes
description to do it.

2. GENTLEMAN  What, pray you, became of Antigonus,
that carried hence the child?

3. GENTLEMAN  Like an old tale still, which will have
matter to rehearse, though credit be asleep and not an
61 ear open. He was torn to pieces with a bear. This avou-
62 ches the shepherd's son, who has not only his innocence,
which seems much, to justify him, but a handkerchief
and rings of his that Paulina knows.

1. GENTLEMAN  What became of his bark and his followers?

3. GENTLEMAN  Wrecked the same instant of their master's death and in the view of the shepherd; so that all
the instruments which aided to expose the child were
even then lost when it was found. But O, the noble combat that 'twixt joy and sorrow was fought in Paulina!
71 She had one eye declined for the loss of her husband,
another elevated that the oracle was fulfilled. She lifted
the princess from the earth, and so locks her in embracing as if she would pin her to her heart that she might no
more be in danger of losing.

1. GENTLEMAN  The dignity of this act was worth the
audience of kings and princes, for by such was it acted.

3. GENTLEMAN  One of the prettiest touches of all, and
that which angled for mine eyes, caught the water though
not the fish, was when, at the relation of the queen's
death, with the manner how she came to't bravely con-

---

52 *clipping* embracing   53 *conduit* structure from which flows water (here
tears)   55–56 *undoes . . . it* renders description incapable of describing
61 *with* by   62 *innocence* simplicity   71 *declined* cast down in sorrow

fessed and lamented by the king, how attentiveness 82
wounded his daughter, till, from one sign of dolor to
another, she did, with an 'Alas,' I would fain say, bleed
tears, for I am sure my heart wept blood. Who was most
marble there changed color; some swooned, all sor-
rowed. If all the world could have seen't, the woe had
been universal.

1. GENTLEMAN Are they returned to the court?

3. GENTLEMAN No. The princess, hearing of her mother's statue, which is in the keeping of Paulina – a piece
many years in doing and now newly performed by that 91
rare Italian master, Julio Romano, who, had he himself 92
eternity and could put breath into his work, would be- 93
guile Nature of her custom, so perfectly he is her ape. 94
He so near to Hermione hath done Hermione that they
say one would speak to her and stand in hope of answer.
Thither with all greediness of affection are they gone,
and there they intend to sup.

2. GENTLEMAN I thought she had some great matter
there in hand, for she hath privately twice or thrice a
day, ever since the death of Hermione, visited that removed house. Shall we thither and with our company
piece the rejoicing? 102

1. GENTLEMAN Who would be thence that has the benefit of access? Every wink of an eye some new grace will
be born. Our absence makes us unthrifty to our knowl- 106
edge. Let's along.      *Exeunt [Gentlemen].*

AUTOLYCUS Now, had I not the dash of my former life in
me, would preferment drop on my head. I brought the
old man and his son aboard the prince, told him I heard
them talk of a fardel and I know not what. But he at that
time, over-fond of the shepherd's daughter – so he then

---

82 *attentiveness* i.e. 'the hearing of it' (Wilson)   91 *performed* finished   92
*Romano* an Italian painter and sculptor who died in 1546   93–94 *beguile . . .
custom* rob Nature of her business, i.e. creating living people   94 *her ape*
Nature's imitator   102 *piece* add to   106 *unthrifty to* failing to add to

took her to be – who began to be much seasick, and himself little better, extremity of weather continuing, this mystery remained undiscovered. But 'tis all one to me; for had I been the finder out of this secret, it would

117   not have relished among my other discredits.

*Enter Shepherd and Clown.*

Here come those I have done good to against my will, and already appearing in the blossoms of their fortune.

SHEPHERD  Come, boy. I am past moe children, but thy sons and daughters will be all gentlemen born.

122  CLOWN  You are well met, sir. You denied to fight with me this other day, because I was no gentleman born. See you these clothes? Say you see them not and think

125   me still no gentleman born. You were best say these robes are not gentlemen born. Give me the lie, do, and try whether I am not now a gentleman born.

AUTOLYCUS  I know you are now, sir, a gentleman born.

CLOWN  Ay, and have been so any time these four hours.

SHEPHERD  And so have I, boy.

CLOWN  So you have. But I was a gentleman born before my father, for the king's son took me by the hand and called me brother; and then the two kings called my father brother; and then the prince my brother and the princess my sister called my father father; and so we wept, and there was the first gentleman-like tears that ever we shed.

SHEPHERD  We may live, son, to shed many more.

139  CLOWN  Ay, or else 'twere hard luck, being in so preposterous estate as we are.

AUTOLYCUS  I humbly beseech you, sir, to pardon me all the faults I have committed to your worship and to give me your good report to the prince my master.

SHEPHERD  Prithee, son, do, for we must be gentle now we are gentlemen.

CLOWN  Thou wilt amend thy life?

117 *relished among* rendered acceptable   122 *denied* refused   125 *were . . . say* i.e. might as well say   139 *preposterous* (he intends 'prosperous')

AUTOLYCUS  Ay, an it like your good worship.     147

CLOWN  Give me thy hand. I will swear to the prince thou
art as honest a true fellow as any is in Bohemia.

SHEPHERD  You may say it, but not swear it.

CLOWN  Not swear it, now I am a gentleman? Let boors   151
and franklins say it, I'll swear it.     152

SHEPHERD  How if it be false, son?

CLOWN  If it be ne'er so false, a true gentleman may swear
it in the behalf of his friend. And I'll swear to the prince
thou art a tall fellow of thy hands and that thou wilt not   156
be drunk; but I know thou art no tall fellow of thy
hands and that thou wilt be drunk. But I'll swear it, and
I would thou wouldst be a tall fellow of thy hands.

AUTOLYCUS  I will prove so, sir, to my power.

CLOWN  Ay, by any means prove a tall fellow. If I do not
wonder how thou darest venture to be drunk, not being
a tall fellow, trust me not. Hark! The kings and the
princes, our kindred, are going to see the queen's pic-   164
ture. Come, follow us. We'll be thy good masters.     165

*Exeunt.*

\*

*Enter Leontes, Polixenes, Florizel, Perdita, Camillo,*   V, iii
*Paulina, Lords, &c.*

LEONTES

O grave and good Paulina, the great comfort
That I have had of thee!

PAULINA          What, sovereign sir,
I did not well, I meant well. All my services
You have paid home. But that you have vouchsafed,     4
With your crowned brother and these your contracted
Heirs of your kingdoms, my poor house to visit,

---

147 *an it like* if it please   151 *boors* peasants   152 *franklins* small land-
owners, farmers   156 *tall . . . hands* bold fellow, quick to act   164 *picture*
(the statue is later said to have been painted; see V, iii, 47–48, 81–83)
165 *good masters* benefactors
V, iii Within the house of Paulina   4 *paid home* rewarded handsomely

7    It is a surplus of your grace which never
8    My life may last to answer.

LEONTES                    O Paulina,
We honor you with trouble. But we came
To see the statue of our queen. Your gallery
Have we passed through, not without much content
12   In many singularities; but we saw not
That which my daughter came to look upon,
The statue of her mother.

PAULINA                    As she lived peerless,
So her dead likeness, I do well believe,
Excels whatever yet you looked upon
Or hand of man hath done. Therefore I keep it
Lonely, apart. But here it is. Prepare
19   To see the life as lively mocked as ever
Still sleep mocked death. Behold, and say 'tis well.

        *[Paulina reveals] Hermione [standing] like a statue.*
I like your silence; it the more shows off
Your wonder. But yet speak; first, you, my liege.
Comes it not something near?

LEONTES                    Her natural posture!
Chide me, dear stone, that I may say indeed
Thou art Hermione; or rather, thou art she
In thy not chiding, for she was as tender
As infancy and grace. But yet, Paulina,
Hermione was not so much wrinkled, nothing
So aged as this seems.

POLIXENES                    O, not by much.

PAULINA
So much the more our carver's excellence,
31   Which lets go by some sixteen years and makes her
As she lived now.

LEONTES                    As now she might have done,

---

7 *surplus . . . grace* additional show of your kindness  8 *answer* repay in
kind  12 *singularities* rarities  19 *lively mocked* vividly imitated  31 *lets
go by* i.e. indicates the passage of

So much to my good comfort, as it is
Now piercing to my soul. O, thus she stood,
Even with such life of majesty – warm life,
As now it coldly stands – when first I wooed her!
I am ashamed. Does not the stone rebuke me
For being more stone than it? O royal piece,                    38
There's magic in thy majesty, which has
My evils conjured to remembrance and                          40
From thy admiring daughter took the spirits,                   41
Standing like stone with thee.

PERDITA                                And give me leave,
And do not say 'tis superstition, that                          43
I kneel and then implore her blessing. Lady,
Dear queen, that ended when I but began,
Give me that hand of yours to kiss.

PAULINA                                O, patience!
The statue is but newly fixed, the color's
Not dry.

CAMILLO
My lord, your sorrow was too sore laid on,
Which sixteen winters cannot blow away,
So many summers dry. Scarce any joy
Did ever so long live; no sorrow
But killed itself much sooner.

POLIXENES                              Dear my brother,
Let him that was the cause of this have power
To take off so much grief from you as he
Will piece up in himself.                                       56

PAULINA                            Indeed, my lord,
If I had thought the sight of my poor image
Would thus have wrought you – for the stone is mine –
I'ld not have showed it.

LEONTES                        Do not draw the curtain.

---

38 *piece* i.e. piece of sculpture   40 *conjured* summoned   41 *admiring* won-
dering; *spirits* life-giving elements   43 *superstition* (an allusion to Protestant
attack upon kneeling before images of the Virgin)   56 *piece up* make up

**PAULINA**
60   No longer shall you gaze on't, lest your fancy
    May think anon it moves.

**LEONTES**                Let be, let be.
    Would I were dead, but that, methinks, already –
    What was he that did make it? See, my lord,
    Would you not deem it breathed? and that those veins
    Did verily bear blood?

**POLIXENES**             Masterly done.
    The very life seems warm upon her lip.

**LEONTES**
67   The fixture of her eye has motion in't,
    As we are mocked with art.

**PAULINA**              I'll draw the curtain.
    My lord's almost so far transported that
    He'll think anon it lives.

**LEONTES**            O sweet Paulina,
    Make me to think so twenty years together!
72   No settled senses of the world can match
    The pleasure of that madness. Let't alone.

**PAULINA**
    I am sorry, sir, I have thus far stirred you; but
    I could afflict you farther.

**LEONTES**            Do, Paulina,
    For this affliction has a taste as sweet
    As any cordial comfort. Still methinks
    There is an air comes from her. What fine chisel
    Could ever yet cut breath? Let no man mock me,
    For I will kiss her.

**PAULINA**          Good my lord, forbear.
    The ruddiness upon her lip is wet;
    You'll mar it if you kiss it, stain your own
    With oily painting. Shall I draw the curtain?

**LEONTES**
    No, not these twenty years.

---

**60** *fancy* imagination  **67** *The fixture . . . in't* the eye, though fixed (stationary), seems to move  **72** *settled* calm, sane

PERDITA                          So long could I
Stand by, a looker on.
PAULINA                          Either forbear,
Quit presently the chapel, or resolve you                    86
For more amazement. If you can behold it,
I'll make the statue move indeed, descend
And take you by the hand. But then you'll think –
Which I protest against – I am assisted
By wicked powers.
LEONTES              What you can make her do,
I am content to look on; what to speak,
I am content to hear, for 'tis as easy
To make her speak as move.
PAULINA                          It is required
You do awake your faith. Then all stand still;
Or those that think it is unlawful business                  96
I am about, let them depart.
LEONTES                          Proceed.
No foot shall stir.
PAULINA              Music! Awake her, strike!
         [Music.]
'Tis time; descend; be stone no more; approach;
Strike all that look upon with marvel. Come,
I'll fill your grave up. Stir, nay, come away;
Bequeath to death your numbness, for from him             102
Dear life redeems you. You perceive she stirs.
         [Hermione comes down.]
Start not; her actions shall be holy as
You hear my spell is lawful. Do not shun her
Until you see her die again, for then
You kill her double. Nay, present your hand.              107
When she was young you wooed her; now in age
Is she become the suitor?
LEONTES                          O, she's warm!

86 *presently* at once; *resolve* prepare   96 *unlawful* i.e. because of the help
of evil spirits   102 *him* i.e. death   107 *double* a second time

  If this be magic, let it be an art
  Lawful as eating.
POLIXENES   She embraces him.
CAMILLO
  She hangs about his neck.
113 If she pertain to life, let her speak too.
POLIXENES
  Ay, and make it manifest where she has lived,
  Or how stol'n from the dead.
PAULINA      That she is living,
  Were it but told you, should be hooted at
  Like an old tale; but it appears she lives,
  Though yet she speak not. Mark a little while.
  Please you to interpose, fair madam. Kneel
  And pray your mother's blessing. Turn, good lady;
  Our Perdita is found.
HERMIONE    You gods, look down,
122 And from your sacred vials pour your graces
  Upon my daughter's head! Tell me, mine own,
  Where hast thou been preserved? where lived? how
    found
  Thy father's court? For thou shalt hear that I,
  Knowing by Paulina that the oracle
  Gave hope thou wast in being, have preserved
  Myself to see the issue.
PAULINA     There's time enough for that,
129 Lest they desire upon this push to trouble
130 Your joys with like relation. Go together,
131 You precious winners all; your exultation
132 Partake to every one. I, an old turtle,
  Will wing me to some withered bough and there
  My mate, that's never to be found again,
  Lament till I am lost.

---

113 *pertain to life* belongs with the living 122 *graces* blessings 129 *upon this push* at this point 130 *like relation* similar account 131–32 *your exultation . . . to* share your joy with 132 *turtle* turtledove (a symbol of faithful love and of sadness)

LEONTES                O, peace, Paulina!
Thou shouldst a husband take by my consent,
As I by thine a wife. This is a match,
And made between's by vows. Thou hast found mine;
But how, is to be questioned, for I saw her,
As I thought, dead, and have in vain said many
A prayer upon her grave. I'll not seek far –
For him, I partly know his mind – to find thee
An honorable husband. Come, Camillo,
And take her by the hand, whose worth and honesty
Is richly noted and here justified                    145
By us, a pair of kings. Let's from this place.
What! look upon my brother. Both your pardons,
That e'er I put between your holy looks                148
My ill suspicion. This your son-in-law
And son unto the king, whom heavens directing,
Is troth-plight to your daughter. Good Paulina,
Lead us from hence, where we may leisurely
Each one demand and answer to his part
Performed in this wide gap of time since first
We were dissevered. Hastily lead away.        *Exeunt.* 155

145 *justified* vouched for    148 *holy* chaste    155 *dissevered* separated

# FOR THE BEST IN PAPERBACKS, LOOK FOR THE

In every corner of the world, on every subject under the sun, Penguin represents quality and variety—the very best in publishing today.

For complete information about books available from Penguin—including Pelicans, Puffins, Peregrines, and Penguin Classics—and how to order them, write to us at the appropriate address below. Please note that for copyright reasons the selection of books varies from country to country.

**In the United Kingdom:** For a complete list of books available from Penguin in the U.K., please write to *Dept E.P., Penguin Books Ltd, Harmondsworth, Middlesex, UB7 0DA*.

**In the United States:** For a complete list of books available from Penguin in the U.S., please write to *Dept BA, Penguin*, Box 120, Bergenfield, New Jersey 07621-0120.

**In Canada:** For a complete list of books available from Penguin in Canada, please write to *Penguin Books Canada Ltd, 10 Alcorn Avenue, Suite 300, Toronto, Ontario, Canada M4V 3B2*.

**In Australia:** For a complete list of books available from Penguin in Australia, please write to the *Marketing Department, Penguin Books Ltd, P.O. Box 257, Ringwood, Victoria 3134*.

**In New Zealand:** For a complete list of books available from Penguin in New Zealand, please write to the *Marketing Department, Penguin Books (NZ) Ltd, Private Bag, Takapuna, Auckland 9*.

**In India:** For a complete list of books available from Penguin, please write to *Penguin Overseas Ltd, 706 Eros Apartments, 56 Nehru Place, New Delhi, 110019*.

**In Holland:** For a complete list of books available from Penguin in Holland, please write to *Penguin Books Nederland B.V., Postbus 195, NL-1380AD Weesp, Netherlands*.

**In Germany:** For a complete list of books available from Penguin, please write to *Penguin Books Ltd, Friedrichstrasse 10-12, D-6000 Frankfurt Main 1, Federal Republic of Germany*.

**In Spain:** For a complete list of books available from Penguin in Spain, please write to *Longman, Penguin España, Calle San Nicolas 15, E-28013 Madrid, Spain*.

**In Japan:** For a complete list of books available from Penguin in Japan, please write to *Longman Penguin Japan Co Ltd, Yamaguchi Building, 2-12-9 Kanda Jimbocho, Chiyoda-Ku, Tokyo 101, Japan*.

# FOR THE BEST LITERATURE, LOOK FOR THE

☐ **A SPORT OF NATURE**
*Nadine Gordimer*

Hillela, Nadine Gordimer's "sport of nature," is seductive and intuitively gifted at life. Casting herself adrift from her family at seventeen, she lives among political exiles on an East African beach, marries a black revolutionary, and ultimately plays a heroic role in the overthrow of apartheid.

354 pages     ISBN: 0-14-008470-3

☐ **THE COUNTERLIFE**
*Philip Roth*

By far Philip Roth's most radical work of fiction, *The Counterlife* is a book of conflicting perspectives and points of view about people living out dreams of renewal and escape. Illuminating these lives is the skeptical, enveloping intelligence of the novelist Nathan Zuckerman, who calculates the price and examines the results of his characters' struggles for a change of personal fortune.

372 pages     ISBN: 0-14-009769-4

☐ **THE MONKEY'S WRENCH**
*Primo Levi*

Through the mesmerizing tales told by two characters—one, a construction worker/philosopher who has built towers and bridges in India and Alaska; the other, a writer/chemist, rigger of words and molecules—Primo Levi celebrates the joys of work and the art of storytelling.

174 pages     ISBN: 0-14-010357-0

☐ **IRONWEED**
*William Kennedy*

"Riding up the winding road of Saint Agnes Cemetery in the back of the rattling old truck, Francis Phelan became aware that the dead, even more than the living, settled down in neighborhoods." So begins William Kennedy's Pulitzer-Prize winning novel about an ex-ballplayer, part-time gravedigger, and full-time drunk, whose return to the haunts of his youth arouses the ghosts of his past and present.

228 pages     ISBN: 0-14-007020-6     **$6.95**

☐ **THE COMEDIANS**
*Graham Greene*

Set in Haiti under Duvalier's dictatorship, *The Comedians* is a story about the committed and the uncommitted. Actors with no control over their destiny, they play their parts in the foreground; experience love affairs rather than love; have enthusiasms but not faith; and if they die, they die like Mr. Jones, by accident.

288 pages     ISBN: 0-14-002766-1

# FOR THE BEST LITERATURE, LOOK FOR THE

☐ **HERZOG**
*Saul Bellow*

Winner of the National Book Award, *Herzog* is the imaginative and critically
acclaimed story of Moses Herzog: joker, moaner, cuckhold, charmer, and truly
an Everyman for our time.

342 pages     ISBN: 0-14-007270-5

☐ **FOOLS OF FORTUNE**
*William Trevor*

The deeply affecting story of two cousins—one English, one Irish—brought
together and then torn apart by the tide of Anglo-Irish hatred, *Fools of Fortune*
presents a profound symbol of the tragic entanglements of England and Ireland in
this century.     240 pages     ISBN: 0-14-006982-8

☐ **THE SONGLINES**
*Bruce Chatwin*

Venturing into the desolate land of Outback Australia—along timeless paths, and
among fortune hunters, redneck Australians, racist policemen, and mysterious
Aboriginal holy men—Bruce Chatwin discovers a wondrous vision of man's
place in the world.     296 pages     ISBN: 0-14-009429-6

☐ **THE GUIDE: A NOVEL**
*R. K. Narayan*

Raju was once India's most corrupt tourist guide; now, after a peasant mistakes
him for a holy man, he gradually begins to play the part. His succeeds so well that
God himself intervenes to put Raju's new holiness to the test.

220 pages     ISBN: 0-14-009657-4

---

# FOR THE BEST LITERATURE, LOOK FOR THE

☐ **THE LAST SONG OF MANUEL SENDERO**
*Ariel Dorfman*

In an unnamed country, in a time that might be now, the son of Manuel Sendero refuses to be born, beginning a revolution where generations of the future wait for a world without victims or oppressors.
464 pages    ISBN: 0-14-008896-2

☐ **THE BOOK OF LAUGHTER AND FORGETTING**
*Milan Kundera*

In this collection of stories and sketches, Kundera addresses themes including sex and love, poetry and music, sadness and the power of laughter. "*The Book of Laughter and Forgetting* calls itself a novel," writes John Leonard of *The New York Times*, "although it is part fairly tale, part literary criticism, part political tract, part musicology, part autobiography. It can call itself whatever it wants to, because the whole is genius."
240 pages    ISBN: 0-14-009693-0

☐ **TIRRA LIRRA BY THE RIVER**
*Jessica Anderson*

Winner of the Miles Franklin Award, Australia's most prestigious literary prize, *Tirra Lirra by the River* is the story of a woman's seventy-year search for the place where she truly belongs. Nora Porteous's series of escapes takes her from a small Australia town to the suburbs of Sydney to London, where she seems finally to become the woman she always wanted to be.
142 pages    ISBN: 0-14-006945-3

☐ **LOVE UNKNOWN**
*A. N. Wilson*

In their sweetly wild youth, Monica, Belinda, and Richeldis shared a bachelor-girl flat and became friends for life. Now, twenty years later, A. N. Wilson charts the intersecting lives of the three women through the perilous waters of love, marriage, and adultery in this wry and moving modern comedy of manners.
202 pages    ISBN: 0-14-010190-X

☐ **THE WELL**
*Elizabeth Jolley*

Against the stark beauty of the Australian farmlands, Elizabeth Jolley portrays an eccentric, affectionate relationship between the two women—Hester, a lonely spinster, and Katherine, a young orphan. Their pleasant, satisfyingly simple life is nearly perfect until a dark stranger invades their world in a most horrifying way.
176 pages    ISBN: 0-14-008901-2

# FOR THE BEST IN HISTORY, LOOK FOR THE